Aunt Bev's Ghost

a novella by

Ron Reed Smith

ISBN: 9798878268721

Table of Contents

Chapter 1 – Old Faces

Daisy's two-day drive back to Cade Valley had been tiring, but at least she had made it in comfort and style. She might have felt a bit guilty about winning John's brand new sixty-thousand dollar pick-up truck in the divorce settlement, but after all, he was the one who decided to spend his evenings with a floozy when he had a beautiful thirty-two-year-old wife at home. Curvy and blonde, she had done everything she could do to save the marriage, but some men are just pigs, and can never find satisfaction in monogamy.

She knew the first stop would be at Janey's Diner for a chicken salad sandwich and slice of her "world-famous" chocolate pie, Daisy's two favorite menu items during her high school days. After a long reunion hug with the motherly cook, she sat down in the corner booth, and the two of them talked for a while.

"So, what's the plan, Missy? You back in town for good, then? I mean, I'm glad you came home, but there probably aren't a lot of openings for financial advisors in Cade Valley."

"Yeah. I know. That job wasn't all beer-and-skittles, anyway. I ended up with a pretty nice bundle from Dr. John, the Womanizer, so I'm not in a panic about that for now."

"Got somewhere to crash? It's just me and the parrot. We've got a spare room that you're welcome to."

"No thanks, Janey. Nice of you to offer. I'm gonna fix up Aunt Bev's empty house. I know it's gonna need a lot of manual labor, but I'm actually looking forward to doing some cleaning and repair work...you know...good old get-your-hands-dirty type therapy. I'm going to drive out there next, and figure out what I'll need from the hardware store."

"Do they rent bulldozers? That place is a mess. And they say...well..."

"They say what?"

"Oh, nothing. Just some wild ideas around town that your Aunt haunts the place."

"Janey! Who says she's dead?"

"Well, Hon, she just vanished into thin air four months ago, and didn't leave a single trace."

"Oh, you know Aunt Bev. She's always been the type to just do what she wants. There's a good chance she headed out West to take care of those two lazy brothers of hers."

"And just left the house and all her belongings? Let me ask you, Child. When is the last time you talked to your Aunt Bev?"

"Well, she called me back in January, and told me that she was fed up with the way Belinda was treating her, and since I already owned Mama's half of the old family place, she was just going to go ahead and put my name on the deed as sole owner of the house and the land."

About that time, another familiar face walked up to the booth. "As I live and breathe...if it ain't Daisy...uh...Hawkes, right?"

Daisy was less than pleased about the big man's interruption. "Oh, hello, Mars. And the last name is Conroy again, if it's any of your business."

Marcus "Mars" Maxton was like so many of those guys who never got past those high school glory days. He maintained the swagger and pride of the teenage all-conference quarterback, but was still doing menial labor in his father's scrap iron yard at age thirty-two.

Discovering Daisy's new situation, he invited himself to sit next to her in the booth. "So...come back home to see who's still available, then?" he asked, with a wicked smile.

"Janey and I were having a private conversation, if you don't mind."

"Easy there, Sweet Thing. This is old Mars you're talking to. You and me...we've got a history. We had a fire going before graduation, as I remember."

"Don't get your hopes up, Mars. I was stupid once. I wouldn't make that mistake twice."

“Ahhh, now. Come on, Daisy. We just had a misunderstanding back then, when we were young and didn’t know any better.” He got uncomfortably close and slipped his arm behind her shoulders. “What say I take you out for a nice dinner this evening, and then we can have a little quiet time for a proper reunion.”

She just ignored him. “Janey, can you get my check?”

“On the house, Missy. And grab that sack of sandwiches on the counter.” Then the waitress gave a sideways glance at the arrogant old football player. “Those are for supper, so you don’t have to settle for any other offers.”

Daisy drove out to the edge of town, to the tired old two-story farmhouse she remembered from her childhood. She found Aunt Bev’s hidden key, walked in, and discovered that the place was in a greater state of disrepair than she had anticipated. “Well, Girl...roll up your sleeves, there’s work to be done.” She decided to start by scrubbing the kitchen and then moving on to finding a clean place to sleep that night. Everything else would have to wait.

Elbow-deep in soapy water, she heard a knock. She answered the door to a meek-looking fellow in dress slacks and a polo shirt with some kind of business logo on the pocket.

“Yes?”

"Daisy? Daisy Conroy? It's you...right?"

"Uh-huh. Do we know each other?"

"Oh, Daisy...Come on! It's me. It's Charles...Charles Worman!"

"Charles....uh...oh, wait. You're Worm, right?" She was proud of herself for remembering.

"Yeah, well actually, that name went away a long time ago. Anyway, I heard you were back, and I thought you might want to catch up with an old flame. We were, after all, quite the couple during those high school days."

"Well, now hold on there, Slim. I remember more than you think. I don't believe anyone would have considered us a 'couple.' If my memory is correct, we just had that one date...um...let's see...the Snowball dance our Junior year...and my mom talked me into that one."

The little guy smiled. "You know, you might not have thought about that night very much since you've been gone, but it was the high point of my four years of high school. Oh, I admit it, you were one of the cool kids, and I was a late-bloomer. But, I believe I've made up for lost time."

"You talking about the pencil mustache? Yeah...congratulations."

He took her sarcasm in stride. "Well, no. You see, Daisy, I've become one of the top representatives for Fuller Realty over in Bristow. I cover all of the west side of the county, including our own little Cade Valley." He looked around to the acreage that surrounded the weathered old house. "In fact, that's what brings me out here today. I was wondering if we couldn't get together sometime soon and talk about a unique opportunity I have in mind for this place."

"What kind of opportunity?"

"Oh, well...you see, this place never did go over very well as a farm, or even for pasturing cattle, for that matter. So, for agricultural use, it doesn't have much worth. But, I've talked to my boss about an idea for a residential development project, complete with paved roads and curbs, lighted streets, a clubhouse and swimming pool, horse stables, a ball park, a driving range..."

"Whoa, whoa, whoa, there Wormy! First of all, the place is not for sale. It's been my family's homestead for over one hundred and thirty years, and as long as I'm around, it's going to stay that way. Capische?"

The nerdy little man was unfazed by Daisy's push-back. "Look, I'm sure this is such a new idea to you that it's kind of uncomfortable to talk about right now. Let's have a nice dinner this evening, after you've had time to give it some thought. I'm sure we can find some way to agree on things. After all, you could get a nice little payday, the town would have a nice new neighborhood, and maybe you and I could re-kindle some flames...if you get my drift. It would be a win-win-win."

She let him finish, and then said, "Maybe I didn't make myself clear. This place is not for sale. Get lost."

He tried once more. "Oh, but Daisy. Look all around you. The place is a shambles. It's not a home for a princess like you. How long do you propose to stay here? Forever?"

"Well, at least until my Aunt Beverly returns...then we'll see."

"And if she never comes home? What then? You know, Daisy, I re-checked the records at the courthouse this morning, and was surprised to find that you are now listed as the sole owner of the property. You wouldn't need her permission to sell it at all, even if she were to return...which I suspect is not gonna..."

She got angry enough to interrupt again. "Why does everyone keep saying that?"

"Sure you won't change your mind about dinner?"

"Head out, Little Man. You're getting on my nerves."

It was about four in the afternoon when Daisy finished making her list of supplies that she would need from Franklin's Hardware Store. Wood glue, screws, nails, hydrant washers, light bulbs, a new electric drill, about four gallons of wall paint...the list would get longer, but this would let her get started.

"Hi, Mr. Franklin. Long time, no see."

"Ahh! Daisy! Just as pretty as ever. Glad to have you back in town. How can I help you?"

"Oh, I've got a list."

He looked at her slip of paper. "Sure thing. Let me gather up some of this for you, and I'll have Jentz load the paint cans in your vehicle."

A few minutes went by, and she saw a man carrying the white paint out to her truck. She thought to herself, "Wow...they didn't have specimens like that when I lived here." A man about six feet tall with sandy brown hair, probably in his late twenties, Jentz Randall was indeed what many females would have referred to as eye candy. On this particular day, he was wearing jeans and an old sleeveless flannel shirt that was probably one size smaller than it should have been. Of course, this managed to showcase the worker's broad chest, and the muscles of his arms...not the large round bumps that one might see on a weight lifter. He reminded her more of a mountain lion, a body possessing speed and power at the same time...the kind of strength that comes from hard work, rather than from hours in a gym. She was kind of in a trance before she finally heard him speak.

"Miss...um, Miss Daisy?"

"Oh, sorry. Did you say something?"

"I just said that I put the cans of paint in the back of your truck out there. Is that okay?"

"Absolutely!"

"Nice rig, by the way. Looks new. Did you pick it out?"

The trance had returned. He had a voice that was a clear as a church bell on a hill. His eyes were as bright green as an Irish meadow, a solid chiseled chin that...

"I asked, "Did you pick it out?"

"Oh, sorry again. Having trouble concentrating today, for some reason. But, no I didn't. It was my husband's choice...uh...I meant to say my EX-husband's choice." The emphasis would have been obvious to anyone in the room.

"Well, it's my favorite shade of red."

"Excuse me for not introducing myself...I'm Daisy Conroy."

"Oh, I know that. We were in Mrs. Mitchell's geometry class together back in high school. I sat two seats back and to the left of you, the side closest to the window. You were a senior and I was a sophomore."

"You remember that kind of detail."

It embarrassed him, but he said, "Sure do." There

was an awkward pause, and then he said, "I'm Jentz Randall. Well...back then, I went by my full name...Jenson Randall."

"You're Jenson? I remember you, too, then. But I don't recall you looking like...well...um...like this."

He blushed. "Nope. Boot camp helped out there. And, of course, hauling bath tubs and air conditioners for Uncle Ray burns off enough to let me indulge in cheeseburgers and milkshakes a few times a week."

"Looks nice...I mean, uh...well, that's nice." She stole one more up-and-down glance at the handsome guy before deciding it was time to leave. "Okay...so, I need to head out. I'll probably see you again. Tomorrow maybe?"

"Looking forward to it."

She had one of the sandwiches Janey had made her for supper, resting in the glider on the front porch, and enjoying the quiet countryside. She thought back over the day, about all the old faces that had reappeared since she had arrived back in town. "Two jerks and a dreamboat. I suppose it could have been worse."

And then she noticed something out on the edge of the property. An old black cat seemed to be stalking her from the tall weeds. She rose from her spot to walk out and investigate, but before she could reach the end of the sidewalk, the cat had vanished.

Chapter 2 – What's All This about a Ghost?

Daisy had found a place to sleep in the spare bedroom of her Aunt Bev's empty house. Of course, the bed was not as big as the one in the master bedroom, but she wasn't quite ready to act like anything more than a guest in the house, in spite of the fact that her name was on the deed. She had been too tired from her first day back in town to wash and dry sheets, so she just unrolled her sleeping bag on top of the bed, and coiled up tightly inside, trying to forget any of the suggestions that the house might be haunted.

When morning came, she slipped on some work clothes. There would be a lot of cleaning to be done before the place was fit for human occupation. She sipped her morning coffee, and then decided to head back in to town. Her plan was to visit briefly with Sheriff Lundy about Aunt Beverly's disappearance, and then stop "conveniently" by the hardware store, where she might catch Jentz on his break, and strike up another friendly conversation.

"Hello, Sheriff. Thanks for giving me a few minutes of your time. I'm sure you have a lot of places to be, right here in the middle of the week."

"Never too busy for you, Miss Daisy. How can I help?"

"Well, Sir...I certainly don't want to come off

sounding critical, but I'm just wondering what work has been done by you and your staff to locate Aunt Bev. Now that I'm back in town, I intend to do some research of my own, and I would rather not duplicate leads that your department may have already investigated."

"Sure, Daisy, sure. No offense taken at all. I'm sure you realize that your aunt and I were good friends...in fact, when Mary and I got married, back in the Dark Ages, your Aunt Bev was the maid of honor. So, needless to say, I've been very concerned about her unexplained absence since it all began a few months ago. I asked Belinda some questions, to see if her mother had mentioned heading out for an extended vacation, or going out to Oregon to help take care of her brothers, but...well...it was my understanding that your aunt and your cousin were somewhat estranged. So, I didn't get any good information from her. I asked if she wanted to file a missing persons report, and she just said that she would think about it. To date, she has done nothing along those lines."

Daisy was not surprised. Her ne'er-do-well cousin Belinda had been a trouble-maker since childhood, and her failing to cooperate with the police department was completely predictable.

"Sounds like Belinda, all right."

"So, from a legal standpoint, I'm hog-tied. Can't

do a lot without the MP report in-hand. And then...well...I'll tell you, Daisy. I just don't have the personnel right now to do a lot of footwork. Me and the two deputies in there, we've got our hands full with traffic, and domestic disputes, and...well, you know."

"Sure, Sheriff. I understand. I'm going to do some asking around, though."

"Do what you need to, but don't put yourself in any kind of danger. If you find anything worth looking at, or if you need our help, just let us know."

Next stop was Franklin's Hardware Store, presumably to pick up some closet shelf brackets. "Hey there, Daisy! Something you forgot to pick up yesterday?"

"Good morning, Mr. Franklin." She was looking around as she answered his question. "I found out the clothes pole in my closet was about ready to fall apart. Looking for some brackets."

"I'll find you a couple." He continued to watch her actions, and then smiled and said, "If you're looking for Jentz, he's been unloading a truck out back."

"Oh...why, no... just..."

About that time, Jentz came walking through the back entrance, and headed right for Daisy. "Hey! You're back!"

"Yep. Might as well get used to it. I need to make that house out there liveable again, and there is a discovery process for each room. Today, it's bedroom closets. Tomorrow...well, who knows?"

"Sure. I understand that. Look, whatever it is you need, just give us a call, and I'll bring it out there personally the first break I get."

"Can't ask for better service than that."

The two walked on down the wire and conduit aisle, perhaps to have just a bit more privacy. "So, if you don't mind my asking...how did you sleep last night?"

"Oh, it was okay. I was so worn out from the drive down here, and from the kitchen clean-up, that I dozed right off."

"So...this might sound strange...but you didn't see anything weird out there, did you?"

"What? Like you mean my Aunt Bev's ghost? That seems to be a pretty popular legend around town."

"Oh, I know. And I don't mean to imply that your aunt is...well...I mean..."

"Dead? Yeah. I don't think we know enough yet."

"Right. And people like to tell stories, don't they?" The young man reached into his back pocket for a business card, and handed it to her. "So, I have to deliver some supplies over to the grade school before noon, but...this has my cell phone number. You know, if you do see anything creepy, or just need some reassurance, call me directly. I'm not Superman or anything, but if you're the damsel in distress, I'd gladly come out to the house as soon as I could."

She giggled, and tapped her forefinger onto Jentz' chest. "Not Superman, huh? You kind of look like him." He just smiled and blushed. She was charmed by his humility, among other things.

There were also stops by the bank, the grocery store, and filling station before heading back home. On the drive back out to the farmhouse, she noticed a young lady walking along the side of the gravel road. It was Belinda.

She pulled up and rolled down the window. "Get in, Belinda. I'll take you wherever you need to go." The younger cousin climbed into the pickup. Daisy noticed that she was the same old Belinda...natural beauty, shapely form, but, good grief...why had no one ever taught that little urchin how to dress? What a shame...so much potential. But here she was, as scruffy as always, a lovely princess dressed in dirty blue jeans, an Aerosmith tee shirt, and a pair of flip-flops that had worn out completely two summers earlier.

"Thanks, Daisy. I heard you were back. In fact, I was walking out to the farmhouse to visit with you."

"Okay. So start visiting."

"Ah...still that same old stuck-up cousin, I see. Is that the way it's going to be?"

"Well, I'm sorry. But let's face it, Belinda. We've never been too close, have we?"

"Not in the past. But after you hear what I have to say, you'll have a little more respect for me."

Daisy pulled the truck up in the drive, and the two of them walked up to the front steps. At that point, the younger woman stopped in her tracks. Daisy shook her head disapprovingly. "Well...come on...let's go in and drink an iced tea and you can tell me what your big news is...you know, the stuff that's gonna make us 'like sisters' again?"

"Ohh...no. This is far enough. I'm not going inside that house. Daisy, I don't think Mom's coming back...not in flesh and blood, that is."

"Oh, spare me. Are you going to start telling me ghost stories like everyone else?"

"It's true! Why do you think I don't ever come around here?"

"Probably because Aunt Bev kicked you out."

"Daisy, I think you ought to unload this place and get out of here. Something's not right. And besides, I heard some big shot realtor was offering a pretty penny for this place. And that's the good news I was talking about. I figure we could get a nice selling price, maybe even a half million. Now, even if it's divided between the two of us, that would be a nice little bank roll."

"Wait, wait, wait, wait...did you just say 'the two of us?' Let's get a few things straight. First, we are not going to talk about Aunt Bev in the past tense. Second, Wormy Worman has not made any kind of an offer, let alone five hundred thousand dollars. Third, if he did offer to buy it, I wouldn't sell it. And lastly...even if I did sell it...notice I said 'I'...you wouldn't get a dime. You buttered your bread on the wrong side for years, and when your mother got tired of it, she put my name on the deed. So, Little Lady, you're barking up the wrong tree."

At this, Belinda stormed off out into the yard, and then turned back. "You'll be sorry about this, Daisy. Bad things happen to greedy people. Don't come looking to me for help when some spirit torments you in the middle of the night!"

None of this surprised Daisy. Her younger cousin had been a drama queen and a conniver for as long as she could remember.

Later in the afternoon, she washed some bed sheets, and hung them to dry on the old clothes line in the side yard. As she worked alone, she felt the hair on her arms standing up. It felt as though she was being watched. From the corner of her eye , she happened to see the weeds move out by the edge of the property, just like the day before. "Here, kitty!"

She thought she saw a small pair of black pointed ears sticking through the honeysuckle vines on the fence, but couldn't be sure. "Oh, well. I suppose you'll come around when you're ready."

It was about midnight when Daisy was awakened by what she thought sounded like someone coughing...or, rather, trying to stifle a cough. It seemed to have come from the side yard, just under her bedroom window. She quietly slipped out of bed, and looked over the sill to the moonlit ground below. Everything had grown eerily quiet, and she couldn't see much of the yard because of the overgrown crab apple tree that was in the way. She held her breath and listened silently for a couple of minutes. Then, hearing nothing more, she went back to bed. "Holy smoke, Girl. You see one black cat, and you start to believe all those weird stories about 'the ghost of Aunt Bev." She turned her pillow over to the cool side, fluffed it up a bit, and dozed off.

Chapter 3 – A Face in the Storm

For the next few days, Daisy never even left the property. There was all that cleaning and painting and repair work to be done, so she busied herself by tackling one room at a time, and doing what she could to make the place more home-like. She had saved Aunt Bev's room for last. If the old widow did, by any chance, happen to show back up while Daisy was there, she didn't want her to feel violated by noticing that someone else had gone through her belongings.

As she swept and cleared out the clutter, her mind ran over all the conversations from her first few days back in Cade Valley. She thought it was strange that so many around town had bought into the story that her aunt was dead and still lingering around the old house in the form of some unhappy spirit.

Since she hadn't checked her for mail for a while, Daisy cleaned herself up a bit after lunch and drove into town.

Just by chance, if you could call it that, she met up with Jentz while she was checking her post office box. It seemed like a serendipitous meeting, although it has to be noted that the post office is just catty-cornered from the hardware store. And, she had actually driven around the block a couple of times, until the new red pick-up could be conspicuously parked in one of the front spots.

"Hey there, Mr. Jentz! Fancy meeting you here."

"Well, I had to come over and buy some stamps for the store. And when I saw the truck, I decided it might be a good time."

After exchanging a few pleasantries and talking about her repair projects for a few minutes, the discussion eventually circled back around to their high school years.

"So...you actually remember where we both sat in Mrs. Mitchell's classroom?"

"More than that. I remember when we got to work together on a team that was trying to calculate the volume of one of the Great Pyramids."

"Wow...I don't remember that. Did we get close...to the right answer, I mean?"

"Oh, I don't know. We passed the class though, right?"

"So...if you don't mind my being nosy...what did you do after high school? I mean, I can't believe I didn't take notice of the likes of you way back when."

"Doesn't surprise me. I was kind of short until after graduation. I grew up a little bit during an eight-year hitch in the Marines. I tried life in the big city for a couple of years...didn't care for it. So, I've been helping out Uncle Ray lately."

"Okay...shut me up if I am asking too much...and I'm just guessing here...but since we've become reacquainted, I haven't heard you mention a Mrs. Randall. Is there someone like that?"

"Nope. It's just me. You know, Daisy, I was stationed at Miramar and Pendleton and even at Quantico for a while. And my buddies always wanted to take me out to the towns and meet the ladies...even had one who claimed his sister and I would be a perfect match. But none of them seemed right for me. It just seemed like they were all glitzy and had dresses slit up to here...lovely women...but nothing I would want to be tied to forever."

"You were smart, Superman. I can tell you. Once you're there, and then find out that you are miserable, breaking it all off can get messy."

"I'm sorry you had to go through that."

"Thanks. But onward and upward, right? I mean...let's talk about more pleasant matters. Like what do you do for fun?"

"Oh...I fish."

About that time, Sheriff Lundy came into the building to check his mail, and happened to spot the couple chatting. "Hi, there, Kiddos. Pardon the interruption, Daisy, but I just thought of something I should have told you about the other day when you were in my office."

"What's that?"

"Well, during those years that you were away, the State came in and built a mental rehabilitation center on the next property over from yours...an institution. It's not a big place. You can't really see it from the road. And they have custodians for their 'guests,' but once in a while, one of them will walk off-property, and it seems like they tend to wander in the direction of your Aunt Bev's house pretty often."

"I haven't seen anyone, Sheriff. Are you saying they might be dangerous?"

"Well, not generally. But there is one troubled young man that has been collected over by your fence line quite a bit. Uhhh...Ira Berry is his name. He's usually okay as long as he stays on his meds, but he got transferred to the clinic because he beat up on a few family members."

"Should I be worried?"

"Probably not. I just wanted you to know about all that, in case you did see someone around the place."

"Thanks, Sheriff. I'll keep that in mind."

When she got back to the farmhouse, she noticed that there was a white SUV in the circle drive. It had a "Fuller Realty" logo on the side.

"Oh, boy. Here we go again."

She left the truck and found Worm waiting for her to return. He was seated in the center part of the porch glider, comfortably sprawled out, with both arms stretched along the back. He didn't offer to get up when she approached the steps, but began another conversation as if the two were still long-lost lovers. "Ahh, the beautiful Daisy, returned from town to her countryside palace."

"What do you want, Worm?"

"Just wanted to have another chat with you about this quaint old farm cabin." And with that he reached over his head without looking, and rapped three times against the glass pane of the window. "I thought maybe you might have had time to think some more about our discussion from the other day, especially now that you've spent a few days trying to repair all the things that need to be fixed. Come and have a seat beside me here, and we'll get into the juicy details about my idea for the land."

"I'm fine right here."

"Come on, Daisy. Don't be that way! I'm not really the Charles Worman you remember from Cade Valley High. That guy was just a wimply little boy with no aspirations, no future..."

"And no upper lip."

"Funny. What I was going to mention was that I have a great deal more to offer now."

"Really? Like what?"

"Well...some ladies find wealth and business finesse quite desirable characteristics in men. Don't let my physical stature keep you from seeing my more attractive traits."

The sarcasm kept flowing. "Thanks. I'll keep that in mind."

"Well, if that's not the kind of conversation you prefer, let me get right down to business. I've been talking with my boss over in Bristow, and I believe we have come up with an offer that you will find most generous...especially considering how delapidated this house has become, and how poor the land is for general farm purposes. What if I were to suggest a number somewhere north of two hundred thousand dollars? What would you say?"

"I'd say that you were trespassing on private property, and that you are officially being asked to leave."

"Ah, come on, Sweetie. You're talkin' to an old boyfriend here. And, I think you'll find out that the salesman's life has made me more determined than ever to get the things I want. You can't just scare me off with words."

"Well, if you're gonna make me call the sheriff, I will."

"That old coot? He ought to be in a nursing home. Has no business wearing a badge. When you talk to him, ask him about the stuff that got stolen out of my car a while back...right in front of my house. He's busy drinking coffee and eating pie at the diner, while I'm losing a gun, a bottle of twelve-year-old scotch, and eighty bucks."

"Maybe you should have locked your car."

"Locked, like it always is...but those idiot policemen couldn't even find a single print."

Daisy really couldn't have cared less. "Look, Worm, I've already told you. The place is not for sale."

"Oh, it's for sale. We just haven't done enough haggling to come up with a price that works." He stood up, and crowded the pretty woman's space, and slipped into what he thought was his Casanova personality. "And actually, I'm rather enjoying the negotiations."

About that time, Daisy heard what sounded like the screen door to the back porch slamming shut. She looked that direction, and then had a "what-in-the-world-was-that look" on her face.

Charles just smiled. "See what I mean? A little bit of a breeze, and this house sounds like it's gonna fall apart."

"You can just let me worry about my noisy old house."

"Well...just a reminder...tornado watches out this evening. If this place blows away, my offer is probably a lot more than what the insurance company will pay out." And with that, the annoying little man ambled off the porch and headed for his car. He turned back for one last unsettling comment before driving off. "Maybe Aunt Bev will 'spook' you into seeing things my way."

Oh, how she despised that conceited salesman. She mumbled to herself as he left the gate. "Hmm. A generous offer, huh? That's a lot less than my dumb cousin guessed...not like I'd accept it anyway."

By now, it was late in the afternoon. As Daisy headed back into the house, she noticed that the northwest horizon had become quite dark, and that the wind was starting to gust a bit harder. She turned around to see if she could spot the black cat that had been hanging around out at the edge of the property. She knew he couldn't hear her, but she said, "Might want to come up to the porch this evening, kitty. Looks like there could be some weather moving in."

The drop in temperature made Daisy decide on a nice hot bowl of tomato soup for supper. After that, as she wandered upstairs to the bedroom, she happened to notice that the door to Aunt Bev's room had been left ajar. "I don't remember that door being opened." She went into the room, and found the closet door the same way. She looked through the closet, which was still full of Aunt Bev's dresses and tops, but nothing appeared to have been disturbed.

On the floor of the closet, however, she noticed a couple of photo albums. She had seen them a few days earlier, but was too busy at the time to look through them. She sat on the bed, turned the pages, and studied all of those old yellowed family snapshots, many of which included images from her own childhood. Toward the back of the book, there were some more recent photos of the family...Aunt Bev with Uncle Ed, just before he passed away...Aunt Bev with all of the members of her bridge club, having lunch at the diner...and one that required closer examination. There, seated on the sofa in the living room, was Aunt Bev with what was obviously a pet...a black cat with a white spot right at the top of his head. She looked up to think. "No...could that be the same...?" She walked down to see if there was any chance that her four-legged stalker had made his way to the porch. He had not.

A bright flash of lightning hit the western sky, and a loud boom of thunder rattled the old house just a second later. The wind picked up, and leaves off the trees and debris from the yard began to pelt the side of the house. "Brace yourself, Sweetie," she told herself. "This one is going to be a dinger." It only took a few more minutes before the hail and the rain began to come down in sheets, so loud that Daisy could hardly hear herself think.

She buried herself into the old musty armchair

that set next to the bed in her aunt's room, hoping that the storm would pass quickly and not do any damage to the farm before it moved on to the east. And, if the lightning and thunder weren't unnerving enough, the electricity suddenly went off. She wrapped herself up with a quilt from the closet and just sat there, trying to be calm.

But things went from bad to worse. There was a pounding at the front door downstairs, and she heard a female voice cry out, " DAISY, DAISY! YOU HAVE TO LEAVE! YOU HAVE TO GET OUT! NO ONE TOLD YOU TO COME BACK! NO ONE TOLD YOU..." and then the yelling tailed off. She ran downstairs as quickly as she could and looked out the window of the door. And there, about fifty feet away in the yard, she saw a creepy image when the lightning flashed. It appeared to be a small woman drenched in rain, wearing a plaid dress and clutching the collar of a tan-colored rain coat. None of the other features of the woman, except for her general build, were obvious. It was too dark to make out the face. The woman said nothing more. She shuffled off to the west, in the direction of the barn, and disappeared behind some old bales of hay.

Could it be? Could that be the apparition that everyone in town was so nervous about? The drenched phantom had already disappeared from view, but Daisy opened the door and yelled, “AUNT BEV! IS THAT YOU?”

But there was no answer to be heard...only wind and rain.

Chapter 4 – The Lazy W

The morning after the storm, Daisy went out to see if anything had been damaged. Fortunately, apart from finding some fallen tree limbs, and some scattered papers from a trash bin that was blown over, the place was pretty much unscathed. She started picking things up.

Her peaceful chore was, however, interrupted by the unbearably loud sound of a car's engine headed up the gravel road. It was a 1971 Chevy Malibu with a forest green paint job. She found it kind of hard to believe, but she recognized both the car and the driver. Mars Maxton pulled up in the circle drive, where Daisy was standing, and revved the engine a few times, just as a way to show off. He rolled down the window.

"Ooooeeee! Don't think I ever saw anyone look that good with a rake before. You certainly know how to wear a pair of jeans, Girl."

She was less than impressed with his crude manner. "You know, Mars. I was doing just fine until you pulled up."

He revved the engine again. "Remember this sweet ride? Maybe you got time to go for a little spin."

"Well, I'm not necessarily surprised that you still drive the car you drove in high school. Seems pretty par for the course. But, I'll give you credit. It looks like you've taken care of it."

"Oh, yeah. This is my treasure...my baby. It's definitely been a chick magnet for me over the years...sort of a good luck charm, if you know what I mean. So, you wanna hop in and let me show you a good time?"

"Uh...no."

"Don't know what you're missing. The Mars Man and his Big Green Cruiser...well, we're kind of a legend in these parts."

"Hmm...sounds kind of made-up to me. Tell you what, though, there is something you could show me."

"Anything you want, Girl. Anything at all."

"I'd really like to see what those tail lights look like when they're headed down the road, about forty miles an hour. Think you could demonstrate that for me?"

"Just as sharped-tongued as ever, aren't you, Daisy. And after I went to all the trouble of coming out here to check on you...the storm last night, and all."

"I'm fine."

"One of them kind of nights when that old aunt of yours walks around the yard spooking the neighborhood...the old bitty."

"Nice thing to say. I take it you didn't care for

my Aunt Bev."

"My first year of junior college, me and Hank Swaim were kind of out celebrating a football win. I had just broken the school record for most touchdown passes in a single game. Anyway, we come driving around up this way, and I dodged a deer, but ran my car through your aunt's and uncle's fence. Hit a couple of their steers, and they had to be put down."

"Dodged a deer? Sounds like there might have been some adult beverages in the cup holders."

He didn't answer that. "Anyway, your aunt calls the sheriff, and they haul me in, without even a breathalyzer test. School kicks me off the team. I lose my scholarship, and missed any chance I had to go to the pros."

"Yeah. I'm not sure you can blame that on her."

"Well, don't you catch on? For the price of two stinking cows, which were gonna get butchered anyway, the NFL lost a future Pro Bowler. So...you don't think I've had the right to be bitter all these years?"

"I think you've shifted blame all these years."

"I hated that old woman. And so did a lot of other people in this town."

He paused for a second, and changed his tone when he remembered why he had come by.

"But that's all ancient history. Let's talk some

more about you and me. You know, we made a pretty handsome couple back during our senior year. I believe we were meant to be together."

"Well, as I recall, Mars, that's the same thing you said to Victoria Wynne, to Jacqui Montez, and to Stephanie whats-her-name...the one with the big...the one with all the curves."

"Aww...they were never you, and you know it. It was always us. Star quarterback and the captain of the cheerleaders...just like out of a movie."

"You really mean that?"

"Absolutely."

"Well...Victoria was the cheerleading captain. I was President of the Spanish Club."

"Ooh. Awkward, huh?"

The old jock, destroyed and embarrassed, revved the engine one more time, and then headed back down the dirt road.

Daisy spent the rest of the day hammering some loose nails and applying a fresh coat of paint to the porch posts. Along about four o'clock, her work was again interrupted, but this time by a much more welcome visitor.

Jentz pulled up and got out of his truck. "Hard at it, I see."

"Oh, well...you know...slow and steady wins the race. Picked up tree limbs this morning, and spent the rest of the day working on the house." She didn't mention that she had been bothered by the old football jerk.

He pointed to the pile of branches that she had pushed to the corner of the yard. "I can help you haul those off, if you want. There's a burn pile down on Gene Crossley's property next to the river. He wouldn't mind if we added what you've got there."

"Sounds great. Let me go wash some of this paint off my hands, and I'll be right back down." She returned to the yard a bit later, perhaps a bit more spruced up than just having cleaner hands. By that time, the hardware man had loaded all of the limbs in the bed of this pick-up and was ready to haul them off.

Just as the couple tossed the last of the broken branches onto the burn pile, they noticed that it had suddenly gotten dark. They sat on the tailgate to rest for a few minutes, and looked up to the open sky.

Daisy commented on the sight. "Wow! I had forgotten how beautiful the stars can be when you get away from streetlights. See right there? That's the Big Dipper...and there's Cassiopeia...and there's..."

"There's what?"

"Cassiopeia...uh...the Lazy W."

"Oh...why didn't you say that in the first place?"

She was still looking to find other constellations

when she said, "So, Jentz...what do you see?"

No answer, so she looked over at him. He wasn't looking at the stars. He was looking at her face.

"I'm not sure. Is there a constellation that looks like the most beautiful woman in the world?"

"Oh...you are a smooth one."

They both laughed.

"You know, Daisy. I gotta be honest. I'm out here in the middle of nowhere, all alone with the girl I've had thoughts about for over twelve years. I'd be a fool not to try and kiss you right now."

She smiled, and answered, "So why don't you?"

Their faces drew very close, and he said softly, "Well, to be honest, because I'm soaking wet with sweat, and I probably reek like an old hound dog."

"Oh, just shut up and kiss me..." And with that she wrapped her arms around the handsome man's head and the two enjoyed a kiss that was long and deep. And when they finally came up for air, she looked at him and giggled. Then she put her forefinger on the tip of his chin and said, "...Hound Dog!"

Chapter 5 – Strange Note

After a strenuous day of yard cleaning and porch painting, Daisy had assumed that a full night's rest would come easily. It didn't. She laid awake and stared out the window, wondering if Aunt Bev, in some form or another, would make another late night appearance. It seemed that, after dark, when she was alone in the house, almost every little creak of a board spooked her. It was hard to rest when whe was constantly listening for coughs and footsteps.

Eventually, though, she was able to settle down by concentrating on more pleasant thoughts, like the tender kiss from the handsome young man with strong arms and a gentle demeanor. She felt better knowing that he was only a phone call away. She must have finally dozed off about midnight.

The next morning, the sun was bright, and the air was crisp. She took a hot cup of coffee out to the glider on the porch, and began to notice all of the painting spots that she had missed the day before. She heard a slight rustling of the leaves that had piled up by the steps. A little furry head popped up, and she heard a loud meow. "Well, hello there, kitty. I've been wondering when you might decide to come and visit the new owner of the property." The cat meowed again, but maintained his distance.

Still, he was close enough for her to notice a prominent white spot, about the size of a quarter, right on the top of his head...the same markings that she had seen on the pet that was in the photo with Aunt Bev. “Okay...so you’re the one.”

Daisy slowly leaned forward in the glider, trying not to scare the skittish animal. Still, he wouldn’t allow her to get too close. “So, what do you want, buddy? You hungry?” She stood, and the black cat headed out toward the west part of the property. She followed at a leisurely pace, but lost track of him as soon as he got to the tall weeds just beyond the main barn. She looked for about thirty minutes, but didn’t find him again. So she returned to the house.

Reaching for the screen door, she noticed that a white envelope had been shoved into the loop of the handle. “Well, that wasn’t there a few minutes ago.” Inside, she found a folded piece of paper with a threatening message. “Hmmm...looks like someone has been playing with scissors.” With letters and words from magazines glued in place, the menacing message read:

“GeT out OF That House, and get OUt of this TOwN. You R Not welcome. U will NOT SurVive. ThiS is YOUr Last warnING !”

“Okay, I suppose it’s time to go see the sheriff again.”

She stopped briefly at the hardware store to bring

Jentz up to speed on the events. He insisted on escorting her to the sheriff's office. The policeman looked over the paper carefully. "You got this today?"

"I can tell you within thirty minutes when it arrived...hand-delivered when I was out chasing a cat."

"Well, I'll dust it for prints, but I doubt if it has any, other than where you touched it. If someone has taken the time to make an art project like this, they've probably been smart enough to wear gloves."

"Why would someone go to all that trouble when it's so easy to print things out these days?"

"Dramatic effect, maybe. Got your attention, didn't it?"

"Oh, yeah."

"That's what they were after. Look, Daisy, I hate to sound like some old grandpa here, but I don't think we can take this too lightly. I mean, someone has gone to great lengths to threaten your life."

"Oh, believe me, I know."

"You got any protection out there?"

"What...like a gun?"

"A gun...maybe a dog."

"I've got a nine millimeter...and I keep it loaded."

"Okay. I really think this is just a scare tactic.

Someone wants you away from that house for some reason. Just in case, I'll have the deputies take a drive out past there once in a while."

"Thanks, Sheriff."

Jentz had remained quiet as long as he could stand it. "Daisy, you're not staying out at the farm tonight. Uncle Ray has a spare bedroom at his house, and he would agree with me that you need to stay with him until we can figure out what's going on."

"Thanks, Superman. I appreciate the offer. But no one is going to bully Daisy Conroy. That's my home and that's where I am going to go. Whoever delivered that envelope had to have watched me walk out to the pasture to look for the cat. If they really wanted to do me harm, they could have just ambushed me when I came back to the house. They didn't do that. Like some coward, they just left a note in the door."

"But, Daisy..."

"But Daisy nothing. End of discussion."

Daisy stopped by the diner for a bite to eat, and to unload some of her new-found worries on Janey. Besides being one of her family's oldest and most trusted friends, Janey knew just about everyone there was to know in Cade Valley, and might be able to give her some ideas about who could be causing all the trouble.

“What can I get you, Missy?”

“Oh...how about a chef salad and a Coke.”

“Shot of cherry syrup in the Coke?”

“Better make it a double. I’ve had a bad morning.”

She proceeded to tell her about the hate mail that had been placed in her door, and also mentioned that she had seen an unexplainable vision the night of the storm.

“Well, I don’t know about the letter. But you know, I told you there had been some tales around town...folks supposedly seeing a woman traipsing around that house of yours after dark.” The kind waitress shook her shoulders. “Brrr...gives me the creeps.”

As she was finishing her brunch, Daisy was approached by a young lady that she did not know. Perhaps a few years younger, the girl was a brunette of striking beauty. She was dressed to the nines, with a tight pair of designer jeans and a blouse that was cut low enough to be alluring to any male in sight.

“Pardon me. Just curious. Are you the divorcee that just moved into Beverly Tipton’s house out toward D Highway?”

To Daisy, this sounded like a legitimate question and a slam all at the same time. “That’s me. How can I help you?”

"Daisy...is it?"

She nodded yes.

"Um. You know, rumors have a way of spreading quickly in a small town like Cade Valley, so I'm not sure what I've heard is exactly the truth. I thought you might be able to clear things up for me."

"About what?"

"Well, about the interest you might have in a certain hardware store employee...who shall, for now, remain nameless."

"Who? You mean old Ray Franklin? Listen, Sweetie, he's old enough to be my grandfather. Besides he's married."

Janey had been eavesdropping from her spot at the lunch counter, and couldn't help but snicker at Daisy's counter-punch.

"Clever. I think you know I mean Jentz Randall!"

"Oh, you mean the one that shall, for now, remain nameless?"

The pretty young woman had already grown tired of Daisy's witty comebacks. She stomped one of her Chanel slingbacks on the floor in disgust, and moved in face-to-face. A quiet but angry voice said, "Now listen here, MISS Conroy. You come in to town with your big fancy red truck and your..." She pointed to Daisy's bustline. "... your tired old body, and you think you can just take whatever you want. Well, for your information, Jentz Randall is spoken for. There's no way he would ever be interested in someone who apparently can't satisfy a husband. So why don't you just quit bothering him. Otherwise...well...you'll soon find out just who you're messing with here." And with that, the angry girl whirled and left.

Daisy said nothing more until the door slammed shut. But then, she broke out into a smile, and turned to Janey, who had witnessed the entire exchange. "Tired old body?" Both women broke into open laughter.

Janey came over to the booth, and decided to fill in some details. "So, now you've met our one-and-only Greta Barker. She's been fishing for Jentz Randall for two years, but so far, hasn't gotten a nibble."

"That's surprising. She seems to have the right kind of bait."

"Well, there is that."

"Gets flustered pretty easily, though. Is there a brain under that all that make-up?"

"Oh, don't underestimate that one, Dear. She might not be able to swap insults with you, but she is famous for being able to submarine her enemies...an absolute devil at dreaming up lies, and spreading them around. Her dad is the current bank president...she doesn't work...so she has plenty of time for scheming,"

"Yeah, and what's the history there? She and Jentz haven't dated, right?"

"So far, only in Greta's dreams. He's had quite a few bees buzzing around since he returned from the military, but hasn't shown much interest in any of the locals."

Daisy's mind flashed back to the tailgate, the stars, and the warm embrace of two strong arms.

Chapter 6 – Danger on the Midway

The weekend had finally arrived, and Daisy got ready for another day of cleaning and scrubbing...and she was hoping to catch another glimpse of the elusive feline that was always just beyond reach.

Jentz pulled up in his truck, and quick-stepped up to the front door. He peered through the screen and yelled into the house. "Hey! Good-lookin! Ya home?"

"Be right there. I'm opening a can of cat food." She walked past him as she headed for the porch steps. "Trying to win a new friend."

"Any luck yet?"

"Nope. He's come close a few times, like he wants someone to pet him. Then, as soon as I reach his direction, he dashes out to the field by the barn." She placed the open can by the steps. "You do know this is Aunt Bev's cat, don't you?"

"Really? How can you be so sure?"

She opened up the photo album. "See that white patch of fur on this cat's head? Well, old Sneaky-Paws out there in the weeds has the same marking."

"Hmm. That's interesting." He looked out into the yard. "I wonder how he's survived without Aunt Bev around."

"Beats me...lots of mice in the barn, though. Cats

managed to feed themselves a long time before Meow Mix was ever invented."

"I suppose."

"What brings you out this way? You working today?"

"Nope. Told Uncle Ray that I was taking off...that I was taking a pretty woman to the carnival over at the fairgrounds...Founder's Day, you know."

"Oh, right. I had forgotten."

For a second, Daisy thought about her encounter with Greta at the diner. "Just for clarification, I'm the one you're taking...right?"

"Well, of course."

She smiled. "Just making sure. Can you give me a chance to shower and get presentable for public viewing?"

"You look fantastic just as you are, but if you just want to change, I can wait. We just need to make sure we get over to the hot dog stand before they run out of brats."

"Oooh...dining gourmet, are we?"

"Nothing but the best for you!"

It was shortly after a ride on the Tilt-a-Whirl when Jentz and Daisy were accosted by a familiar trouble-maker. Apparently Mars Maxton had begun his Founders Day celebration a bit early.

"Well, if it ain't old Mr. Hardware hisself, makin' a move on the new girl in town." Jentz just grinned, and dismissed the comment as coming from a liquored-up bum.

Daisy was not so willing to let it go. "Look, Mars, here's a reminder. I'm not the new girl in town. I grew up here just like you did." Then she pointed to her escort. "And for that matter, just like he did."

"Oh, sure, sure, sure, sure, Sweetie. We're all just a bunch of chums...just like when we were all together on the playground at school." He began to sing the school fight song, "Green and Gold, Green and Gold, Filled with Spirit, Forever Bold..." Then he paused and chuckled. "Can't remember the rest of it. But we're all pals, right? Once a Bulldog, always a Bulldog!" He laughed loudly, and then threw an arm around Jentz, who carefully pushed it away, trying not to escalate the situation.

"You know, Maxton, I don't mean to seem unfriendly here, but I think you might have had a few too many. Now, why don't you just head over to the bingo tent. They've got some empty folding chairs in the back section. Catch a few winks, and before long, you'll be feeling just fine."

Mars looked past him, and worked his way over to the girl. "Well...what I'd really like to feel is..."

That's as far as it got. Jentz grabbed the old jock by the shirt collar, pulled him up nose-to-nose, and with a calm stern voice, said, "Now, I'm going to talk real plain about this. See? Never....never...never touch her, or even act like you're going to."

"Or what, Big Guy? You gonna do something about it?" And with that the old washed-up quarterback took a wild swing at Jentz, but was nowhere close to landing the punch. The Marine repaid the action with a short jab to Maxton's mid-section, which curled the intruder over at the waist.

Interestingly, the sheriff had been nearby and watched the entire scene play out. He hadn't worried about intervening until Jentz could teach the drunken Mars a lesson. "Everything okay over there, Randall?"

"Just fine, Sheriff...just fine."

"Okay. Let me know if you need anything."

"Thanks."

The hours rolled away as the couple walked the midway together, holding hands, swinging them like a couple of grade-school sweethearts. There were stops for pretzels, snow cones, and cotton-candy-for-one, since the hardware guy had never acquired a taste for it. He explained to her that it was a texture thing.

Just before they got aboard the ferris wheel, Jentz slipped over and talked into the ear of the ride operator. Then the couple got into their private pod, and watched the crowd and the tents get smaller and smaller as their part of the wheel approached the top. The ride stopped, supposedly to let on more passengers, but Daisy seemed to notice that it was taking quite a bit of time.

"Stars again, Daisy. Want to show me where that Lazy J is again?"

"It's a W, Hound Dog." And the stage was set for another magical moment. She cupped the sides of his face with her hands, and opened her lips to his. The kiss may have been even longer than the one at the burn pile.

Finally, the ride began to move again, and it dawned on the pretty blonde that her date had arranged for the long pause at the top, nearest the sky. "You told him to do that, didn't you?"

He just smiled, and said, "Best five bucks I ever spent."

With the evening winding down, they walked out to Jentz' pickup, got in, and started down the driveway back to the main road. As he turned the wheel to turn left, there was a loud CRACK! on the passengers side of the vehicle. He quickly noticed that the glass had shattered. "Daisy, get down!" Then he yanked the truck over to the side, and they both ducked low for a few seconds, trying to understand what had just occurred.

And, of course, Sheriff Lundy made yet another appearance.

"It just popped, Sheriff. Sounded like someone

threw a brick at the truck."

"No, Son, the deputies looked, and they found a bullet hole. Someone out there is serious."

"You're saying someone was shooting at us?"

"No question about it. Deputy Parks and I will stay here and see what we can find, but it's almost midnight, and we may not be able to find any evidence or any witnesses this late. I'll have Briggs follow you two home. If you have any more trouble tonight, don't mess with nine-one-one. Call me directly. You've got my number." Before leaving, they heard the sheriff give an order to the deputy. "Bobby, walk around and see if you can find Mars Maxton. I want to talk to him...tonight."

Chapter 7 – Spot and Ira

In spite of the attempt on the lives of her and her Superman, Daisy still insisted on spending the night in her own home. She just didn't want to let the bad guy think he was winning. She was convinced that if she left the old house empty, someone might come in and ransack the place, or worse...burn it to the ground. She tossed and turned most of the night, but did manage a few naps here and there.

Jentz drove up to her farmhouse fairly early the next morning. He had new locks for the doors, and was going to install them as soon as possible.

"So...you okay?"

"Yeah, still a little rattled, but I piled a couple of chairs in front each door, and went to bed with a handgun and a baseball bat...probably nodded off a little after three. What about you?"

"I drove back to the fairgrounds after dropping you off...just wanted to see if I could notice anything obvious. It was all pretty much locked up, and no one was around. I figured the sheriff wouldn't want me out there making myself a target for the second time in an hour so, I went on home. I slept okay."

"Well, that's good."

"But Lundy was right, when I got in the truck this morning, I noticed a cut on the dashboard of my truck. A bullet was buried in the hole. I took it over to the police this morning."

"You actually found the bullet?"

"Yep. You know, I'm wondering if you should get a dog...not like a chihuahua...but something that can scare off unwanted visitors, or at least keep a bad guy occupied until you can find a place to duck and hide. My brother's got a malamute that he would probably let you keep for a while."

"No. Thanks anyway. If I got a dog, it would probably scare off my other pet."

"You mean that black cat?"

"Yeah. We kind of have an understanding. He agrees to watch over me from the edge of the yard. I agree not to get within ten feet of him. Actually, those are his terms, not mine."

Jentz decided to inject a bit of levity. Maybe it's your aunt, reincarnated...you know, coming back in a different form."

She grinned, but disapprovingly. "Yeah, I don't think so. Remember, we're talking about my Aunt Bev, not General Patton."

"Well, if you change your mind about the dog, let me know."

After lunch, there was a breakthrough with the cat. He finally got the courage to come all the way up to the porch and taste the can of tuna-flavored food that Daisy had set out earlier in the day. And when she went out to see if she could pet him, he actually rubbed against her ankles and purred. "Well, it's about time, Mister. Now, if I only knew your name...well...not like it matters...since cats don't generally come when they're called, anyway. But I have to call you something. How about Spot?" The cat looked up from the plate of food and meowed. "Yeah, I know it's a dog's name, but it fits you so well...that white place on your head and everything."

She sat on the edge of the porch, petting her new friend, and enjoying the sunshine. Eventually, the cat began to wander out toward the west edge of the yard again. But this time, because he had become a little more tolerant of having a human sidekick, she got close enough to watch him go to his path in the weeds. A little farther on, past the main barn, they approached another old outbuilding that had been used when the place was an operational farm. It was pretty close to the west fence line. Daisy had forgotten that it even existed.

Once in view of the little shed, the cat dashed on ahead. By the time she caught up to him, he had reached the old storage building and was being cuddled by a strange man in a blue jumpsuit. He was gently stroking the cat's fur and whispering in its ear.

Daisy thought she might know who this was, and

didn't want to set off any alarms. So, she played it rather low-key. "Well, hello. I see you've met the kitty."

"I feed the cat."

"I'm sorry. What was that you said?"

"I feed the cat...on Sundays at church time...I feed the cat."

"Oh, okay. Well, my name is Daisy. What's your name?"

"I'm Ira. It's Sunday, and there is church going on over at the hospital. So I brought the sausage from my breakfast plate, and came over to feed Mama Burley's cat."

Daisy continued to patronize the visitor. "Well...I think that's really nice of you, Ira. But whose cat did you say it was?"

The troubled young man seemed rather put out that Daisy didn't already know, and disgustedly responded, "Mama Burley. Mama Burley's cat."

"Oh. Ira, you don't mean Beverly's cat, do you?"

"I said...Mama Burley!"

"Okay. Okay. I must not have heard you right the first time. So, Ira...have you seen Mama Burley recently?"

"No. She used to bring me out some blueberry muffins. And then, we'd talk about the cat for a while. And then she'd walk with me over to the fence and make sure I didn't get hurt on the 'bob-wire' part. But she don't do that no more since the Redcoats and the Starman came."

"The Redcoats and who?"

"Starman."

"And who are they...the Redcoats and Starman? Are those some people you know?"

The guest at the mental rehab facility ended the conversation abruptly. "No. They are just Redcoats...and I called the nine-one-one. I called." After this statement, Ira lost his train of thought. "Well, I have to leave now. Preachin' is probably almost over, and I get in trouble with Artie when he finds out I been skippin' church to feed the cat." And with that, he gently set the cat down on the ground, then headed out running for the west pasture, disappearing behind the big grove of elm trees by the corner fence post.

Daisy didn't try to catch the poor fellow. "So, that's Ira."

She thought for the rest of the day about the mental patient's jibberish. She felt uncomfortable that he had referred to Aunt Beverly as "Mama Burley," probably because she remembered that Ira had been institutionalized at the Sapphire Center for beating up his own mother, according to Sheriff Lundy's accounts.

Later that day, she called the sheriff's private number, and relayed details about her happenstance meeting with Ira Berry. She asked if he knew the significance of Ira's story about Redcoats and a Starman.

"Sure don't, Daisy. But I wouldn't worry on it too much. The poor guy is at the State hospital because he is obviously deranged. Who knows what goes on in that peeled little head of his. Redcoats today...Blue horses tomorrow...you just never know what is next."

"I suppose. He just seemed so convinced. I was wondering if you..."

"Nope...let me stop you right there. I know you said you were going to start asking around about your aunt's disappearance, and I said that was okay. But, interviewing a patient with mental problems is over the line. You probably won't get any useful information to begin with, and you might accidentally trigger the guy into some sort of fit. He's at that hospital for a reason, you know. Let's not jeopardize any progress he might have made up to this point. Understand?"

"Sure. I guess I hadn't thought about it that way."

"By the way, where did you say that you found Ira and the cat?"

"At an old out-building that is over on the west edge of the property."

"Hmm...what's in there?"

"Beats me. Looked like it was all locked up. Probably just some of Uncle Eds' farm stuff. I had forgotten that it was even out there."

Chapter 8 – The Diary

Daisy spent the next morning on the phone with the authorities in Eugene, Oregon, identifying herself as a niece to one Berl Tipton and one Paul Tipton, most frequently referred to as Punk. Of course, there were the usual "red tape" questions that police often ask when a completely unknown stranger asks about the information in their files. This seemed to take forever, and Daisy had to talk to at least five individuals before she could find out anything about her long-lost relatives. Eventually, though, she was told that her Uncle Berl had been living on the streets and spending any cash he owned on booze and meth. He had been found dead on a street corner last November, probably due to exposure and pneumonia. Punk was a little less of a trouble-maker, but was nonetheless a familiar character to law enforcement. Unlike his younger brother, Paul had been renting an apartment in a rough section of town, and was killed by crossfire when a gang member tried to get his vengeance on a stool pigeon. Detective Barrows even sent Daisy an electronic file with the latest images (mug shots) of the two Tipton brothers. She was amazed at how old the two men looked, despite being in their late fifties.

"So, Detective, I really appreciate you giving me

this information. But, can you tell me...was there an older woman tending to either of those guys...say...within the last four months?"

"Let me look." He flipped a couple of pages in the report. "Nope. Don't see any record of that."

Daisy dropped by the hardware store to report her disappointing news about the uncles to Jentz. He continued to unload and shelve several boxes of power tools that just been brought in by UPS. As she complained about the amount of time it took just to get what was basically "no new information," he uttered an occasional "uh-huh," or a "sounds about right." It didn't take too many minutes for the blonde beauty to figure out that Jentz did not seem too interested in what she had been saying.

"Pardon me for wasting your time, but I just thought you might be curious about what was going on in Oregon."

"Yeah. I'm just really busy this afternoon."

Now... this she did not understand. The Marine who had been at her side through this whole ordeal was suddenly too involved in arranging Skilsaws and drill bits to give her the time of day. She switched gears immediately. "Okay, Mr. Randall. I'm not stupid. We've been a team now for the past several days, and then, just out of the clear blue sky, I'm being treated like some trouble-making customer. What's going on?"

He finally paused, and leaned against a large cardboard container. "Well, maybe...instead of looking for my shoulder to cry on all the time...maybe you should have the good doctor to be your Superman. He's probably going to want that big red truck back, anyways."

She was totally lost. "Good doctor? What in the world? Are you talking about John Hawke? About the man who just made me waste almost ten years of my life? Is that the one you're talking about? Do you think that I've totally lost my marbles, and would be willing to put in again with that slob?"

"Spoken words can mean one thing, but written words...the ones you have time to think about before putting them on paper...they seem to carry a lot more weight."

"Jentz, You need to help me out here. I have no clue about what you are referring to!"

"Well...let's talk about your diary, shall we? Have you noticed that it's missing?"

"My diary? But I don't..."

"Apparently, when you came in to the post office yesterday, it fell out of the front seat of your big red truck...yep...fell right out onto the street. Then someone picked it up, read some of it, and thought that I might be interested in the last few pages...the ones where you complain about being bored with all this small town stuff...that you're going back to the city to see if John will take you back. That diary."

"Okay. I talk now...and you listen. First, I don't keep a diary. I never have. Secondly, and this is without question the most important point, John Hawke is an evil, narcissistic pig, who subjected me to excrutiating emotional pain for most of the past decade. I fully admit that I'm not the smartest person in the world, but why, in God's Honorable Name, would I ever want to put myself in the clutches of that demon again?"

The hardware salesman had nothing to say in return.

"And, by the way...just where is this 'diary' that suggests my insanity?"

"Daisy, I can only say that it was given to me by someone here in town...someone who thought I was going to be hurt."

"Do you have it?"

"It's in the back."

"Get it."

Daisy read aloud the last two of about twenty-five handwritten pages, all penned in the same handwriting and the same blue ink. Most of the pages were notes about the move back to Cade Valley, the loneliness of a newly-divorced woman in a town she no longer knew, the questions about the sincerity of a certain strong-armed hardware store clerk, and how tired she was from trying to clean up an old haunted house. And then, at the end, the notes suggest that she had made the biggest mistake of her life, and that running after her ex would be the only way all of her problems would end.

After reciting the last several lines, she gave Jentz a stern look, and said, "What...a...load...of...crap."

"So you didn't write this?"

"I'm frustrated. After all this time, how could you even think I was capable of this type of rubbish? Look...I'll say this one time, and then I'm done talking about it...that diary is not mine. It's a forgery...an elaborate one, but a forgery nonetheless."

"Daisy...I..."

"Don't 'Daisy...I' me. I'm ticked." And she stormed out of the hardware store.

She quickly walked down the street and plowed open the front door to the diner. She stomped to a booth and sat down. Janey had no trouble picking up on the mood. "Bad morning?"

With teary eyes, she proceeded to tell the waitress, her loyal confidante, about the fake diary, and Jentz' willingness to believe it.

"Who, Janey? Who would go to all the trouble to concoct a story and write out twenty some pages...wait a minute." She looked up, smiled, and nodded. "This has all the earmarks of one Greta Barker."

"Cade Valley's Miss America strikes again. I told you she was as venomous as they come."

"Well, she doesn't work...unless you call shopping on-line all day a job...and would have had plenty of time to hand-write something that has more pages than War and Peace."

After having a good cry, and finishing off two cherry Cokes, she drove back home. She wasn't sure whether she was mad or sad, although it was probably a combination of the two.

At about eight o'clock, there was a timid knock at the front door. She didn't answer it. A sheepish Jentz Randall said, "Daisy, can I come in and talk?"

"No. I'd rather not do any more talking tonight."

"Daisy...I'm sorry. I should have known."

"Well, you're right about that."

Chapter 9 – The Kitchen Window

Daisy continued to brood about her bad day. Not only had she found out that Aunt Bev was not in Oregon caring for her brothers, but she had also been smeared by the local town gossip.

By eleven o'clock that evening, she had built a little nest on the sofa, complete with a crossword puzzle book, about four editions of her aunt's old People magazines, a seed catalog, and a large mug of hot chocolate. She knew that she wouldn't be able to sleep much that night, and had decided that if she was going to stay awake and fret until the wee hours of the morning, she might as well have something to look at. She thought about adding a glug of schnapps to her cocoa, but the bottle in the pantry was empty.

She sat all alone in the front room. All was quiet, except when the wind would gust, and cause the oak branches to scratch against the siding of the house. It was creepy, but Daisy was so tired that she eventually was able to ignore the creaks and snaps, and she finally dozed off.

And then...BAM. BAM. Two hard blows to the door to the back porch shook the house. She snapped back awake, and had to focus for a few seconds to realize what direction the sound had come from. She threw off the quilt and the magazines, and raced for the kitchen to look outside. The lack of light made it difficult to make out, but there in the back yard...just near the clothes line...she saw the same phantom apparition that scared her so much the night of the big storm. It was the figure of a woman, wearing what looked like a long blue plaid dress, along with a hat and a tan raincoat. The spectre moaned loudly, and then hobbled off into the darkness, toward the barn.

Daisy screamed, and then yelled out, "GET AWAY! JUST LEAVE ME ALONE!"

And then another loud crash was heard...this time from the front of the house. The rooms were completely dark, but Daisy could see the outline of a large man kicking open the door. She let out another scream.

"DAISY! Are you okay?" To her relief, it was the familiar comforting voice of Jentz Randall.

"Jentz! Is that you?"

He rushed over and wrapped his strong arms around her. "It's me, Sweetheart. It's me. Everything's okay."

"But I just saw...well...I'm not sure. I think I just saw Aunt Bev's ghost again...out in the back yard!"

He moved to the window to see if there was anyone still outside in the back. "What did it look like?"

"Same as before...the same kind of dress that my

aunt always wears, and a tan rain coat...just like the one I got Aunt Bev for her birthday last year. Whoever or whatever it was banged on the door, and then shuffled off into the dark part of the yard."

"Well, it looks like they're gone now." And he hugged the shivering blonde even tighter.

"But, Jentz, I don't understand...why were you here? You busted in just a few seconds after I screamed."

"Daisy, I know you said earlier that you didn't want to talk to me. But I just couldn't go home. I couldn't leave here without begging for your forgiveness...without admitting to you how stupid I was to fall for that ridiculous scam. I should have known the words in that diary couldn't have been the truth. I was just an idiot. And I was going to sit on those porch steps all night until I could tell you that.

"Jentz, I just thought we trusted each other."

"It's more than trust, Darling. It's love. Daisy, I want you to know something...something I finally figured out during these past weeks. The reason I've been by myself all these years...never finding someone to marry...it's because ever since I was a sophomore in high school, you've been the only woman I ever wanted. I could never find anyone else as perfect as you. And the thought of losing you, especially if it was because of my own stupidity...well, it's worse than any nightmare I could ever imagine."

She said nothing. Instead, she wrapped her arms around the Marine's neck and kissed him, the way a woman kisses the man she loves. It was late, and they both were tired. Daisy went to bed, and Jentz stretched out on the couch, just in case the stalker in the tan raincoat decided to make another appearance before morning. Fortunately, everything remained quiet.

Sheriff Lundy came out as soon as Daisy had called him about this most recent visitation of the mysterious Aunt Bev. "You know, I hate to suggest this, but I'm not sure we can guarantee your safety out here. Maybe you ought to go off somewhere and lay low for a while. Maybe just head back to the city for a week or two. Then, when things have calmed down a bit, or when I've had a chance to figure out what's going on, you could come back and get your remodeling done in peace."

Daisy had not been defeated by the overnight terrorism. "Nothing doing, Sheriff. No one is running me off. I'm in charge here."

"Well, it was just a suggestion."

Eventually, the two men headed back for town. Sheriff Lundy had to relieve one of the deputies on patrol, and Jentz had to re-stock some shelves at the hardware store.

Daisy was trying to get a little rest, and had been joined by the black cat as she sat on the front steps of the porch.

"I hate that cat." The voice was both familiar and unpleasant.

"What do you want, Belinda?"

"Nothing, really. Just out for a stroll, and thought I would stop by and check on my lonely cousin."

"Lonely?"

"Oh...you know...a little bird tells me that you're off to the big city again. Maybe having some second thoughts about leaving your Sugar Daddy."

"Well, you've got that wrong."

The younger woman pulled her hoodie up over her head, and grabbed her own arms as if she just had a chill. "Don't know how you stand it out here. That black cat...my mother's ghost...too spooky to be comfortable."

"It suits me fine. And stop talking about your mother as if she's already dead. That's just disrespectful."

"Oh, come on, Daisy. You know she's not coming back. And she's not gone off to Oregon or Wyoming, or wherever our weirdo uncles live now. If you were smart, you'd sell this place to that Worman guy, and move back to your big-city life...where you belong."

"We've had this discussion before. Remember,

you talked about how we could divvy up the money and live high on the hog? And remember, I told you that you wouldn't get a dime, even if I did sell? Remember all that?"

"Things have a way of balancing out, Miss Daisy. You know it wasn't right for my mother to sign over the property to you without asking anybody."

"Well, Belinda, I think you might have already spent your inheritance on tattoos and bail bondsmen. Aunt Bev probably decided that having your name on a deed would probably mean the end of the family farm legacy."

"Some legacy...pastures that won't grow hay and fields that won't grow soy beans. This all could be a nice new housing project...but no, you have to..."

"Belinda! Why are you so interested in my plans for this farm? Get it through your skull. It doesn't involve you!"

"Well, Cousin, that project is going to happen, one way or the other. If you try to get in the way, it could get dangerous." Daisy just shook her head in disgust as the trampy young lady walked off the property.

Chapter 10 – Sad Discovery

It was the start of another weekend, and the weather had turned a bit colder. A misty fog shrouded the front yard of the farmhouse, and Daisy coaxed the little black cat up to the porch with a few bites of leftover ham. Spot seemed satisfied to sit on the porch for a while, but then began his regular trek out to the west edge of the property. Again, the pet's new owner followed along, presumably to his favorite place, out under the shed on the fence line.

As the weeds got higher, Daisy lectured the cat. "You know, if you would just stay up by the house, I wouldn't have to be worrying about ticks and chiggers." Of course, there was no reaction from the cat, other than to march on to his nest, just underneath the two wooden steps that led up to the door on the shed.

"Okay, you've had your exercise. Let's go back to the farmhouse." Daisy waited for a second, and then turned to head back.

The cat responded with a loud and long meow. The lady stopped to see if the cat was following. "Well...come on." Again, the cat remained in place, but let out with another wailing call.

"Oh, alright. Let's look around and see why you find this shed so special." She took an old dusty oil rag from the hood of the nearby tractor, and rubbed the caked dirt off of the small window that was next to the door of the building. She peered inside. "What is that? Oh, dear Lord! Aunt Bev!" Daisy couldn't see an entire body, but she did see someone's feet and ankles tied together with nylon rope, and extending out onto the floor beyond a stack of five-gallon paint drums. "Aunt Bev! No!"

Jentz got the first call, and followed the instructions to rush out to the farm and bring a pair of bolt cutters that could cut off a dial padlock that had no known combination. A second call summoned the sheriff and his deputies. The four men all arrived at exactly the same time, finding a distraught Daisy sitting on her porch steps and sobbing uncontrollably.

"Why? Why would anyone do that to Aunt Bev?"

A few minutes later, Janey rolled up in her Jeep, and climbed out almost before the vehicle had come to a complete stop, running to the porch to console her young friend. She was there to help Daisy inside as the authorities bagged the body of Beverly Tipton, and transported the deceased to the county morgue.

"What happens next, Sheriff?"

"Well, the way she was found, there is no question that this was a homicide. Mert Wilkins is the county medical examiner. He's out of town until

Wednesday of next week. We'll need to let him do his work before any burial arrangements are finalized. In the meantime, I have a couple of leads I want to run down. I couldn't do it before, because, without a body, we had to assume she had only gone missing. But now the investigation belongs to me and the guys here. You can stand down now, and let us do our job."

Cade Valley was one of those towns where news spreads fast, especially bad news. Before long, there were people dropping by, some of whom Daisy had never even met, to offer condolences. One "mourner" was noticeably absent that day...Belinda Tipton.

Later in the evening, when everyone else had gone, Daisy and Janey sat at the kitchen table of the farmhouse, and began to make funeral arrangements. In spite of the fact that Aunt Bev's disappearance always suggested a possibility that the old woman was dead, and shouldn't have created such a shock, Daisy had difficulty in talking about her aunt in the past tense, and broke up in tears frequently as they wrote out a list of things to do. Jeff Bond, the new young pastor at the Baptist church would be asked to deliver the address, and Lacey Carlton would probably be willing to provide the music for the service. Burial would be at Crescent Ridge Cemetery, in the plot next to Uncle

Ed's grave. An actual date for the funeral could not be determined at this point, since they were unsure how long it would take Mert Wilkins to complete his forensic investigation of the body.

Jentz left the planning to the two ladies, but offered support by keeping their coffee cups filled.

Around nine o'clock, there was another quiet knock. It was Mary Lundy, the sheriff's wife. Mary had been like a sister to Daisy's aunt and her mother over the years, and the two hugged and cried as they met at the front door. "Oh, Sweetheart, I'm so sorry it ended up this way. I loved your Aunt Beverly so much. She and your mom were like family to me."

"I know, Mary. The three of you were together since grade school. They didn't have any better friend than you."

"Listen, child. You've been back here for a few weeks now, and I feel so guilty for not coming out to see how you were getting along. I've just been so busy lately...and now..."

"Oh, Mary. That's no problem. I understand. I figured we'd have lunch sometime soon, maybe after things sort of settled down. And we still can."

Jentz patiently sat in the lounger as the three old friends cried about their recent loss, and laughed about the good old times when life in Cade Valley was less complicated. When Janey and Mary finally left, about eleven o'clock, Jentz gave Daisy a long hug, then cupped her face in his hands and kissed her goodnight on her forehead. He promised that he would check on her first thing the next day. She nodded her head okay, and said that she was tired, and would probably fall right to sleep.

By the time she had gotten into bed, however, her mind began to whirl around a lot of unanswered questions. Who would have wanted to kill her aunt? How did they do it? When did they do it? Had anybody seen it happen? She finally calmed herself down by telling herself that the police would now be doubling down on their efforts to work the case.

On the other hand, while she didn't really believe in ghosts, the fact that the strange visions of the lady in the rain coat had occurred after her aunt had been killed...could it be possible...? "Oh, come on, Daisy. Get ahold of your senses, and go to sleep."

Chapter 11 – The Usual Suspects

Several days had passed since the terrible discovery of Aunt Bev's body. Fortunately, there had been no more ghostly visions in the back yard. The cat had finally abandoned his vigilant watch at the locked storage shed, and spent most of his time in the glider on the front porch of the farmhouse. Jentz was making trips out to check on Daisy at least two or three times a day, and Janey was making sure that she had hot meals and chocolate pie from the diner.

She had been waiting patiently for Sheriff Lundy to report on the progress of his investigation, but so far, he had not given her a call. Eventually, she drove in to meet with him in person. "Hello, Sheriff. I don't mean to bother you, but I was just wondering if you had anything to tell me yet about the leads you were going to follow."

"Well, maybe. I'm not supposed to give out information like this before it's time, but I need to make sure you stay safe. I think there is someone you need to watch carefully, Daisy. If you can keep this to yourself, I'll let you know that I have some suspicions about Charles Worman. I know he's been pestering Beverly for several months now to buy up that property, and has been pretty vocal...shooting his mouth off all around town...that he was going to get that acreage for a real estate project he had dreamed up, and didn't care what it took to get that done. So, that goes to motive."

"Wormy? Listen, Sheriff. I'm no fan of Charles Worman, but I'm not so sure a runt like that could man-handle my Aunt Bev...getting her tied up like that, and all."

"And I'm not sayin' he did. I'm just sayin' that, after a few cans of Michelob down at the pool hall, he bragged that no old woman was gonna stand between him and the things he wanted. Now, your aunt was a good woman, but she had made a few enemies in town down the through the years. Worman's not the only name on my list, but that's the one I'm startin' with."

"Who else?"

"Don't push this, Daisy. Me and the deputies are doin' this methodically. I'll let you know as much as I can, as long as it doesn't jeopardize my chances of catchin' the killer."

"Okay."

Jentz took off work a little early that day, and showed up at the farmhouse with his bass boat in tow.

"What's this?"

"Get some grubby jeans on. We're going fishing."

She wandered out in the yard as he got out of the

truck, and grabbed his arm as they walked up on to the porch. "Uncle Ray give you the afternoon off?"

"Yep. We both agreed that you need a change of scenery for a few hours...get you out of your Nancy Drew mode...let your brain relax for a while."

"Okay, but if we're fishing with worms, you have to bait the hooks."

"Deal."

After they reached the limestone bluffs on the bend of Sapphire River, Jentz tied up to a tree branch to keep them in place. For a long time, there was very little conversation. But after a few catch-and-release opportunities, Jentz noticed that the fishing wasn't as therapeutic as he had hoped, so decided to let Daisy verbalize her thought process, and get things out of her system. "Okay, so go ahead and tell me what you're thinking. You got a suspect in mind?"

"I don't know. I wasn't supposed to say anything, but Sheriff Lundy really has some notions about Wormy."

"That realtor guy we went to school with?"

"Yep."

"He's a mouse. He couldn't have moved your Aunt Bev all the way out to that outbuilding by himself."

"I know. That's what I said, too. I mean, Aunt Bev was not a big woman, but she was no featherweight, either."

"So, does the sheriff think Worman might have had an assistant?"

"He didn't mention one. He just said that there had been some harsh words between The Worm and Aunt Bev, and that he had bragged around town that he knew how to get her to sell the farm. She probably told him to get lost, just like I did."

"Well, I don't know...I don't think Charles Worman would have been the first name on my list."

"So, who would be your prime suspect?"

"Oh...maybe an ex-football jock who had an ongoing war with your aunt ever since his college days. He always did say that Bev and Ed shouldn't have turned him in for that DUI incident. And, if there was anyone around who could move a body all the way from the farmhouse to that shed, it would be Mars Maxton. Get that guy liquored up, and there's no telling what he'd do. You think that wasn't his bullet that almost killed the two of us at the fairgrounds?"

"I admit, he has a temper." She thought for a few seconds and then said, "I just wonder if the sheriff is thinking about Ira...you know, that mental patient over at the state hospital? I mean, he didn't seem like a violent guy, but he apparently has a history."

"Well, hold up now. We don't even know the

cause of death yet. No sense in jumping to conclusions before Mert gets back, and tells us how she died."

"I suppose you're right. We do need more information."

"Just be sure to keep looking over your shoulder for the time being. Whoever did this is still out there, and someone is still trying to scare you off the land. Keep your eyes peeled."

"I will." Daisy scooted over next to Jentz in the boat. "Of course, as long as I have my big strong Marine close by, I feel pretty secure." She smiled flirtatiously, and since it was just the two of them and the birds and the crickets (and the worms), the smile led to a long, passionate kiss.

Jentz finally took a deep breath. "So...are we done fishing?"

"I caught everything I want." She looked up. "Besides, it will be dark pretty soon, and I know of a porch glider that's just perfect for stargazing. Interested?"

"Love those astronomy lessons."

Chapter 12 – Gathering Clues

"I know you have a busy schedule, Dr. Timmons. Thanks for taking a few minutes to talk with me."

"Sure, Miss Conroy. I was sorry to hear about your aunt's death. How can I help you?"

"Well, it's about one of your patients...Ira Berry."

"Oh, yes. I know about him wandering off-base, and ending up on your property. Artie does his best to keep track of everyone, but we've been understaffed for quite some time, and it's difficult to make sure they all stay on the premises. We're set up to operate as a hospital, not a prison. I can talk to Ira, and make sure he understands that you don't want him over there."

"Well, Doctor, I didn't come over here to get Ira in trouble. I mean, he does come over from time to time, but from what I have heard, I think that was just to maybe visit with my aunt, when she was still around, and to bring food to the little black cat that stays around our place. I'm sure that, for his own safety, you don't want him leaving the yard, but..."

"No, that is absolutely correct. All kinds of problems arise when he leaves the hospital grounds, in terms of safety and liability. We'll just have to watch him closer, and keep him contained."

"So, I'm not quite sure if I can ask this, because I know that patient information is privileged, but Ira mentioned some names to me the other day that might possibly be related to my aunt's death."

"Well...feel free to just ask me. If it is something I can answer I will. Otherwise...well, we don't want to violate the HIPAA rules."

"Fair enough. Doctor, Ira told me that my aunt was not around to visit with him lately, ever since the Redcoats and Starman showed up...and he said he had called nine-one-one. I have no idea who or what he was referring to, but there could be some significance to all this."

"Okay, so here is my answer...and I think that it will be within the boundaries of what I am allowed to share: 'I have never heard Ira, my patient, talk about Redcoats and Starman.' That's my statement."

"So, as far as you know, Ira Berry does not have some friends, either real or imaginary, that go by those names?"

"Daisy, I know you want to find out who killed your aunt. And I want to help...believe me I do. But I think you are just going to have to take the statement I just gave you as my final comment on the matter. I would not want anything I say here today to be turned or misconstrued by the authorities, and end up causng my patient to be a suspect in a criminal matter. I hope you can understand that." Dr. Timmons could tell by her expression that she was not completely satisfied with his answer. "And with regard to a nine-one-one call, that's Ira's go-to move when he sees an unattended cell phone. He thinks nine-one-one is the answer to all of his problems. The county operators have gotten to recognize his voice, and pretty much just ignore the calls."

"Of course. Well, I don't suppose you'd let me visit..."

"I'm sorry, but certainly not. No offense, but you don't have the formal training required to interview fellas like Ira. And even if you did, we would need to involve lawyers and mental health specialists...it would be a real spider's web. Now, if the sheriff comes with that same request, I will make the necessary arrangements; but I don't see that being a prudent action at this time. "

"I understand, Doctor. Thanks again for your time."

Daisy made the short drive back to the farmhouse, somewhat disappointed that the hospital staff wasn't willing to ask Ira a few questions about his Redcoats and Starman. After all, she hadn't asked them to hypnotise him or subject him to a polygraph test. She thought that Ira might be able to clear up a few questions without all of the medical and legal mumbo-jumbo.

She pulled into the driveway about the same time that Sheriff Lundy arrived.

"Hello, Miss Daisy. Was out this way on patrol, and thought I might check on you."

"Hi, Sheriff. I'm fine, thanks. Not trying to be too nosy, but is there any new news?"

"Well, maybe. That's another reason I came out. Daisy, let me remind you that I'm sharing details with you that would normally be kept in-office. But Beverly was a close friend, and I just feel like I can trust you with it."

"Sure, Sheriff."

"Okay, so I got the judge to issue a search warrant for the residence of Charles Worman. And this afternoon, Bobby...uh, Deputy Parks...and I went over to take a look around."

"Did you find anything suspicious?"

"Possibly. You see, I just think with all of the bad blood between that realtor fella and your Aunt Bev, he had a motive for murder. Trouble is, we found her all tied up a good eighty yards from the house...and, like we talked the other day, Charles is pretty scrawny to be forcing anything on someone who was putting up a fight. So, that makes me wonder if he killed her...oh, I'm sorry...if her death actually occurred while she was in the house. It's been so long since she disappeared, I don't think we're gonna find a lot of scuff marks, or evidence in the yard that would prove that, but we'll look anyway."

"Oh. Okay."

"Now, Mert still hasn't examined the body, but I know you are worried about all of this, and I thought it might help for you to know that she was not shot...or cut. At least, that's what the deputy and I determined when we bagged the body. So, I went looking through Worman's house for something that might have killed her in a different way...say like, maybe a poison."

"And did you find something?"

"Well, I'm not sure yet, but there was a fairly new bottle of ethylene glycol, about half-full, on the shelf in his garage."

"What's that?"

"Oh, it's a pretty common chemical. It's the main stuff they use to make antifreeze, and brake fluids, and items like that. It's not all that often that you find a bottle of just plain old ethylene glycol in the household, though."

"Poisonous?"

"I did a little reading up on it. It has a sweet flavor to it. If someone was to slip some in your morning coffee on a regular basis, it might not get noticed, but it could eventually be lethal. Now...this is all just speculation at this point, so I don't want you thinking this is exactly what happened. We have a lot of steps in the investigation that haven't been performed. But...I came out here to talk, so you wouldn't think we're sitting back and not doing anything."

"No, Sheriff. I understand. And thanks."

"Oh, and by the way...if I were you, I wouldn't park that shiny red truck of yours in front of the bank. Our little trouble-maker Greta spends a lot of time down there in her dad's office, and she has a bad habit of keying vehicles that belong to folks she doesn't like."

"Well, I'm certainly part of that crowd. I appreciate the heads-up."

Later in the day, Jentz and Daisy were at the diner having Janey's daily special, red beans and rice. While Daisy was absolutely sure that she shouldn't be sharing details about the privileged conversations she had had earlier in the day, both at the state hospital and with the sheriff, she knew she could bounce her ideas off Jentz without them going any further.

"So, the hospital administrator didn't know what Ira meant when he mentioned a Redcoat?"

"No, Jentz. Not Redcoat...Redcoats...plural."

"And Sheriff Lundy still has Worm at the top of his list?"

"That's what he told me."

"Well, here's an idea...and keep in mind this is just me spitballing here...but when the folks from Fuller Realty make those TV commercials, aren't they wearing bright red blazers...with a big F on the pocket?"

It was like a light came on. "OF COURSE! THEY DO WEAR RED COATS!" Daisy suddenly realized how loud her reaction was, and quickly quieted down. "They do wear red coats. That must have been what Ira was talking about, right?"

"Possibly."

"Oh, Superman. You may have just figured out a piece of the puzzle. Now, if we go with Ira's Redcoat comment...and we add in what Sheriff Lundy said about that ethylene google...or whatever...we might come up with a scenario where our old school mate Worman managed to poison Aunt Bev before hiding her out in the shed. I mean...that seems possible, right? And if Ira happened to be out by the shed when all that took place...yeah!"

"Maybe, Daisy...maybe. But here's a problem with that story. Your aunt and Wormy were not what you might call 'best friends.' Not really likely that they had brunch together on a regular basis, where he could sneak something in to her coffee every day."

"No. That's right. And it's also not likely that he

force-fed her a whole half-bottle of the stuff at one setting. So, back to Square One, I guess."

The two of them sat quietly and thought some more.

Then Jentz tilted his head sideways a bit, and added, "Of course, you did say Ira mentioned Redcoats...plural...more than one, right? So, let's go back to that idea about Worman having a helper. Isn't that possible?"

"It's more than possible. It's probable. We just need to figure out who it was. But it sure seems like Old Wormy is the guy."

"Well, don't go making a 'citizen's arrest' without all the facts."

"I won't. But I think I know where to snoop next. Want to drive over to Bristow with me tomorrow?"

Chapter 13 – Let's Check the Map

It was about nine o'clock in the morning when the big red truck pulled in to the parking lot for Fuller Realty in Bristow. After looking around to make sure Charles Worman's vehicle was not there, the two entered the business, posing as a couple looking for a nice spot to build a new home.

"Hi, folks. I'm Brent Fuller. Is there something I could help you with this morning?"

"Well, maybe," said the pretty blonde. "We're not looking to do anything right away, but in a year or two, we would like to locate here in the Bristow area, and wondered if you could recommend a lot that would be good for new construction...maybe something along a river...kind of off the main drag, and with some nice big trees. Can you think of anything like that?"

"Absolutely. I'm sure we can look through the listings and come up with something to interest you." Brent asked them to be seated, while he moved to his desk and started checking his computer. "Uh...let me ask...does it need to be in Bristow? Or maybe just in this area?"

"Not necessarily in Bristow...but something in the county might be good."

"And you're looking at land now, but plan to build later?"

"Exactly."

"I have something here that you might be very interested in, then. It's not in Bristow. It's actually closer to Cade Valley. It's a little pricey for this area, but it is going to be a prime location, and very high in demand by this time next year."

Jentz broke in to the conversation. "You said it was going to be a prime location? Why is it not a prime location now?"

"Well, one of my realtors and I have been putting together a new residential project just north of Cade Valley. It's all laid out on that map on that work table over there. We haven't finished all the land agreements yet, but it promises to be a beautiful neighborhood with all brand new homes, paved roads with curb and guttering, tennis courts, a pool, a driving range...the works. We'll be calling it Sapphire Lake Village."

"Sapphire Lake? You mean Sapphire River, don't you?"

"It's Sapphire River now. We've gotten some information showing where the Corps of Engineers is going to build a dam down at Sherwood...some kind of flood control issue. And when they do, what folks know as Sapphire River in this part of the state will become Sapphire Lake. Of course, there has been no official announcement about the dam...we're just hearing things from some very reliable sources at the state capitol. But believe me, you're gonna want to have a locked-in price on one of those lots over there. It's going to skyrocket when that area becomes a new recreational area.

Daisy responded next. "Wow. How many people know about it?"

"Probably not many. Like I said, it's not a done deal. And quite frankly, if you were anxious to build a house right away, I wouldn't have even mentioned it. But since you're not in a hurry..."

"Yeah...great idea. Thanks, Mr. Fuller."

"Brent."

"Brent. Well, thanks, Brent. Mind if we look over that big map?"

"Oh, please do. Check out the lots on the south bend of the main loop. They are going to be first ones to go, being lakeside, and all. Let me know if you have any questions."

A greedy Charles Worman would not have wanted Daisy or her aunt to have seen the large four-foot by six-foot area drawing that was located in the conference room of the realtor's office. There was information about the speculative project that would have made his attempts to buy Beverly Tipton's farm at a low price almost impossible.

Daisy and Jentz looked over the map and talked in whispers. "Look at this. This shows Aunt Bev's south pasture as being right up on the shoreline of a new lake. That little punk offered me two hundred thousand for the entire farm, and they're probably gonna charge half that much for just a single one-acre lot. The rat!"

"Well, Daisy, this all is based on the idea that the dam downstream actually gets built."

"They think it is. Look at this map. It's not hand-drawn, you know. They've already divided it up in to plots. They've even laid out the streets and named them. Sapphire Drive...Larkspur Circle...Worman Street...OOOH!...and look at this little gem." She pointed to one little spur road that angled off the main loop right down by what would be the new waterfront. "See that?"

Jentz leaned over the table and squinted to see what she was referring to. "Honeybug Road...yeah...so...?"

"Superman, that is a huge piece of the puzzle. Ever hear anyone call bees 'honeybugs?"

"Can't say that I have."

"Pretty unique, wouldn't you say?. But guess what...that little piece of the map just told me the identity of our second Redcoat."

"How?"

"In his younger days, my Uncle Ed was an amateur apiarist, and always had a couple of honeybee hives out back. Dear little cousin Belinda, when she was a toddler, always misunderstood and called them ‘honeybugs.’ Uncle Ed used to think that was cute, so he nicknamed Belinda ‘Honeybug.”

“So you think...”

“Uh-huh. That’s a ‘Belinda’ reference. Old Wormy was naming streets ahead of time. He didn’t just pull that street name out of thin air.”

“Glad you were here to pick up on that one. If Belinda was involved, it can explain how old Charles got close to Aunt Bev’s breakfast coffee on a regular basis.”

As they left the office, Brent waved a friendly goodbye, and said, “Was that map any help to you all?”

“More than you know, Mr. Fuller. More than you know.”

Chapter 14 – The Second Redcoat

Having found proof of Belinda's association with Charles Worman, Daisy and Jentz drove straight to see Sheriff Lundy in Cade Valley, and laid it all out for him.

"Look, Sheriff, I certainly don't take any pleasure in suggesting that my own flesh-and-blood cousin had a part in murdering her mother, but it sure looks like that might be a possibility."

"Yes. Yes, it does. I mean, I've always known about the rift between Beverly and her daughter down through the years. Lord knows I would have written her off long before your aunt did. We've had her in the lock-up several times, but usually for penny-ante stuff...you know, shoplifting, drunk in public, and oh, there was that one time she went joyriding in Mabel Hasbrook's Volkswagen. Of course, we had to let her go on that one because Mabel didn't want to embarrass your aunt around town because of her daughter's stupidity. But, I never thought there was enough hate there to result in a murder."

"Me, neither, Sheriff. But that's what it looks like."

"You wouldn't happen to have any proof of Belinda having that nickname when she was a kid, would you?"

"I don't know. Some of the family scrapbooks are in the top of the closet at the farmhouse. I'll dig through them."

"That might be a good to have."

Jentz reminded Daisy of something. "Tell him about the rain jacket."

"Oh, that's right. When we were driving over here, I remembered that the ghost in the yard, supposedly my Aunt Bev's spirit, has been wearing a tan rain coat each time I've seen it. I had mentioned to Jentz the other night that I recognized that tan coat. I bought one just like it for Aunt Bev for her birthday a year or two ago. And I don't remember seeing it in any of the closets at the house."

"You think Belinda used the coat?"

"Uh-huh. It all makes sense. In the dark, she might have just looked like any old woman. But if she was wearing a coat that I knew to be my aunt's, I would be more apt to think it was a ghost. And, now that there's evidence that she and Wormy were in cahoots, I think I know when she snatched it from the closet."

"When?"

"Right after I came back to Cade Valley, old sly Charles was waiting for me on the porch glider as I drove up one day. He talked about an offer to buy the place, and I remember that he nonchalantly reached over his head and rapped on the front window as we were talking. Right after that, we heard the back door slam. I didn't figure it out until today, but I believe our realtor buddy was 'on look-out' when his partner-in-crime was raiding the closet. When I came up on the porch, he had to signal to Belinda that she needed to head out the back."

"That seems to fit."

"Yep."

"Well, Daisy, you seem to be doing my work for me. But I'll be honest, me and the deputies would never have known anything about that nickname to tie them two together. Tell you what...before you guys leave the office here, let's make a quick call to check on something. I'll put it on speaker, but let me do the talking."

The sheriff looked up the number for Fuller Realty and dialed it in. "Hello, Mr. Fuller? This is Sheriff Lundy over in Cade Valley. Say, I was just doing some background work on a case, and you might be able to help me out with a name that I'm missing."

"I'll do what I can, Sheriff."

"Could you, by any chance, tell me the names of all the female employees you have on staff? Would that be a lot to ask?"

"Well, not at all. It's pretty easy. I don't have

any female employees. I run the office here by myself, and all of our sales agents are male."

"Really. How long has that been the case?"

"Almost forever, I guess." Then a pause. "Well, now wait. A few months ago, Charles Worman tried to get his little girlfriend to become an agent...umm...can't think of her name right now, but that didn't work out. She did a short internship with us, but then couldn't pass the licensing exam."

"Blonde, by any chance?"

"Yes. Not bad looking, either, as I recall. Was she a Betsy...a Brenda maybe?"

"That's okay, Mr. Fuller. I think that gives me the lead I was looking for. Have a nice day, and thanks."

Daisy smiled. "Blonde and couldn't pass a test...that's Belinda in a nutshell."

"Okay, folks. Let me and Parks do some more investigating. I'll keep you posted."

As Daisy and Jentz climbed back into the truck, something suddenly occurred to the hardware worker. "Darn!"

"What is it?"

"Oh...I don't know...I was kind of hoping we could pin this all on a drunken old football player."

"Aww, too bad. You don't always get what you want, now, do you?" They both grinned.

They drove over to the diner to grab a quick

lunch, and to celebrate a successful morning of fact-gathering. Janey's place was fairly busy at this time of the day, and most of the tables were occupied with the downtown regulars. Jentz and Daisy limited their audible conversation to topics like fishing and house repair, since the sheriff had warned them not to say anything, even accidentally, that might tip off the "Redcoats."

As luck would have it, Greta Barker made a grand entrance, noticed the couple in the booth, and decided on an attempt to publicly embarrass her competition. "Hi, Jentz. I see you're still having to 'protect' the scaredy-cat that keeps seeing ghosts all the time."

Jentz looked up at the intruder, smiled, and quickly put his arm around Daisy's shoulder. "Best job I ever had, Greta."

Since that maneuver hadn't worked, she got louder, and directed her next attack right at Daisy. "Oh, and by the way, I spoke with my father...he is the bank president, you know...and he said that it would be a cold day in you-know-where before he would ever take you on as a personal finance advisor. So, if you're shopping around for a job, maybe you should just pack your bags and head back to the city!'"

In spite of the normal lunch-time chatter in the room, Greta's verbal jab was heard all throughout the little diner. And before Daisy had a chance to respond, Ernie Pratt, at the next table over, butted in with his own loud comment. "Hey, Daisy! I need a finance advisor...could you help me out?"

Then June Willis broke in from the corner booth. "No, Ernie...me first. Daisy's gonna work on my finances next."

Another yell came from someone eating at the counter. "Hey, I need help with my retirement plans, Daisy. You can work for me!"

And for the next several seconds, there were "job offers" from all corners being hollered at the same time. This, of course, was all followed by raucous laughter, an obvious rebuke of the prissy Miss Greta...and she knew it. After an angry glare, she stomped a foot, whirled around, and headed for the door.

Daisy, who hadn't said a single word the entire time, just smiled, raised her hand to the diners, and said, "Thanks, everybody."

Chapter 15 – Putting the Puzzle Together

The sheriff and his deputies spent the next few days tying up loose ends on the Tipton murder case.

A hotel clerk in Bristow was willing to testify that he had checked in Charles Worman and a recognizable lady guest at least three times in the past several months, which could prove that the two had secretly been more than just acquaintances for some time.

A preliminary version of the medical examiner's report showed that there was damage to the victim's kidneys that would have been consistent with poisoning by ethylene glycol. And the fingerprint evidence on the bottle that was found in Charles' garage matched police records for Belinda Tipton, as well as one other person, which was assumed to be Worman. The sheriff would be able to verify this as soon as both were under arrest.

The bullet recovered from the padded dash of Jentz Randall's pick-up truck had been examined. It was a thirty-eight caliber, the same size bullet used by Worman's 'supposedly-stolen' hand gun.

An examination of the yellow nylon rope that was around Beverly Tipton's ankles and hands matched a roll that was found in Worman's garage. And in fact, the cut angle on the end of the rope was a dead match complement for the one left on the rope still on the reel.

Paul Carver, who owned the local pool hall, confirmed reports that Worman was a frequent weekend customer at his establishment, a bragger when he was drunk, and was always loud and vocal about knowing how to "run that Tipton witch out of town." He also had given the names of other Friday night regulars who would be willing to provide the same kind of information in court, if needed.

A thorough search of the main barn on Daisy's farm property turned up some old clothing, hidden under a couple of square hay bales in the loft. Of particular interest, there was a wet blue plaid dress, a gardener's hat, a muddy pair of sneakers, and...most importantly...a tan rain jacket. Without mentioning these items, the sheriff had asked some carefully constructed questions of Belinda Tipton, aimed at proving that she was familiar with the current positioning of items in the loft. The prosecutors would want to suggest in court, even circumstantially, that she was hiding her 'Aunt Bev's Ghost' costume somewhere near the farmhouse, so it could be conveniently used and stored whenever necessary.

Brent Fuller was questioned in order to understand what the potential profits would be on the proposed real estate project, if and when the river was dammed up to create a new recreation site on the spot of Beverly Tipton's farm. His answers concerning lot pricing, even when the improvements and amenities were factored in, were staggering. This information could be used to show a jury just how much motive there would have been to acquire the property before the announcement of the Sapphire Dam project was made public.

And then, finally, under the supervision of Dr. Timmons at the state mental hospital, Deputy Parks was allowed to ask Ira Berry a few questions about what the poor soul might have seen during the past few months. A legal transcription of the interview would be entered as evidence during the trial.

"Yep, Daisy. I've been working with the county attorney, and it looks like we have a fairly solid case. Ira said that he had seen two people with red coats dragging your aunt into the shed on one of the Sunday mornings that he had left the hospital grounds to pet the black cat. He says that he got scared and ducked behind those big elm trees in the back corner of the lot. Of course, he told us that he also dialed nine-one-one as soon as he could find a phone to borrow, but he'd made so many of them by that time, the emergency officer pretty much laid off the call when she recognized Ira's voice."

"But, Sheriff...what about Ira's Starman? He mentioned Redcoats, but did he say anything about the Starman?"

"Not to Parks, he didn't. But I wouldn't dwell on that, if I were you. We were looking for Ira's help on the Redcoats and he gave it to us. If we start muddying the water with the rest of his jibberish, we might put his whole testimony in question. If he is called to testify in court, a defense attorney will probably clobber him in cross, but at least the jury will have heard him tell his tale."

"I suppose."

Jentz had been listening in. "So what do you think, Sheriff Lunday? Is there enough to haul them in...Charles and Belinda?"

"As far as I'm concerned...yes. But we're still waiting on Mr. Wilkins' final coroner's report, and then the county attorney will have to give us the go-ahead. I'm figuring that will all be ready by tomorrow afternoon. So...keep everything under wraps for now, but be ready for some fireworks when we make the collar."

Daisy was still concerned. "You brought Belinda in for questions. You don't think she will be suspicious and head out of town?"

"We thought about that before the interview. Two things. First, I don't think she would make any move without Worman telling her what to do. Second, we didn't have the prosecutor in on the interview. As far as she was concerned, we were just going through the motions of standard police work after a homicide...just asking questions. In fact, before she left, she asked if we planned to talk to Mars Maxton about his long-term hatred for her mother. And to play along, we brought him in for a few minutes, just so she would think we were still looking for suspects."

"So, you think they'll both be surprised?"

"I do. And the deputies are on twenty-four hour surveillance for now. We want to know exactly where the two of them are located when the call to execute the arrest comes in."

"Well, Sheriff. I appreciate you sharing all that with Jentz and me. I'll certainly sleep better tonight knowing that we are getting those two idiots behind bars."

"Sure. No problem. Mums the word, Daisy. No slip-ups now that we're this close."

Daisy smiled and used her hand to make a tick-a-lock sign at her lips.

Sheriff Lundy looked over to Jentz. "You know, I think the strain of all this murder investigation stuff is beginning to show on our pretty new neighbor, here. Not much more you two can do to help us out. Why don't you think about taking Miss Daisy out of town for a couple of days. The white bass are running up on Tallman. A little fishing might be a nice little get-away."

Jentz smiled and looked at Daisy. "Sounds like a

good idea, don't you think?"

"Well, I wouldn't mind spending a day or so in the boat...maybe napping instead of fishing...but at least there wouldn't be bothered by a tan rain jacket."

"That's right. And if you all head out today, you can dodge the rain that's movin' in on us."

They left the police station, and Jentz walked Daisy to her truck. She took his arm, and said, "If you don't mind, maybe we could leave for Tallman Lake tomorrow, instead of today. I really need to see that those two are in custody before I can relax much."

"No problem. That would give me a chance to clean up the boat first. Tomorrow afternoon, then?"

"It's a date." She squeezed his arm again. "I'll bring my star maps."

Chapter 16 – The Big Surprise

Finally feeling a little more at ease, Daisy headed to bed a bit early. She reminded herself that the whole mess would be over after one more day, and then fell asleep the moment her head hit the pillow.

At about two o'clock, however, she was awakened by a familiar and unpleasant sound. Just as once before, there were muffled coughs heard out in the yard, and the sounds of footsteps walking near her window, and then trailing off toward the west. At this point, she was more angry than scared. She grabbed her nine millimeter Smith and Wesson, and made sure it was loaded and ready to fire. With one more peek out her bedroom window, she saw the beam of a bright flashlight moving out past the main barn, in the direction of the little storage shed where Aunt Bev's body had been discovered.

She whispered over her phone, "Jentz! Get out here! Someone is breaking into the storage shed."

"I'm leaving now. You stay right where you are!"

But, of course, she didn't. She put on some jeans, a sweatshirt, and shoes, and quietly slipped out the back door. Following the light until it stopped at the little shed, she watched as a large man went inside. It got even brighter, as the intruder apparently lit up one of the kerosene lamps setting just by the door. He appeared to be shuffling around, and searching for something.

Daisy had no idea how long it would take Jentz to arrive, but felt like she couldn't wait much longer if she wanted to catch the prowler by surprise, and discover his identity. Mustering her courage and unlocking the safety on her gun, she rushed to the door, and flung it open. "DON'T MOVE!" And there, to her amazement, stood Sheriff Lundy, holding an old axe handle.

"It's me, Daisy! It's just me!"

"Sheriff? What are you doing here?"

"Looking for one more piece of evidence...found it, too." He held an axe handle up.

Daisy, being one who is hard to bluff, questioned his explanation. "Not at this time of night, you're not. What's really going on?"

The sheriff took on a defeated demeanor. "Okay. Lower the gun and I'll tell you the story."

"Nope. You tell me the story, and maybe I'll lower the gun."

"Fine. I got my advance copy of the medical examiner's report today. The cause of death could have come out one of two ways. In one scenario, Mert could have found that the cause of death was poisoning, and no one would have been surprised. He did find that there was poison involved, but he identified the true cause of death as blunt force trauma to the back of the head."

"What? They poisoned her, and they hit her?"

"No. They poisoned her. I'm the one who hit her...with this." He held up the axe handle, and then pointed to a spot toward the butt. "Of course, by tomorrow evening, I will have coerced my prisoner, one Charles Worman, to put his fingerprints right about here."

"I don't...I don't understand."

"Let me walk it back a ways. Several months ago, probably after she started drinking Belinda's poison in her coffee, your Aunt Bev called me out to the house. She told me that she thought she was dying from stomach cancer, and that she wouldn't last much longer. And then she told me that she couldn't go to her grave without coming clean about a long-kept secret that the two of us had."

"What secret?"

"Well, there was something that she and I knew about, but we were the only ones. As you know, we were very close. Mary and I didn't have no better friends than your aunt and uncle. But...and this just happens sometimes...one afternoon many years back, Bev and I sneaked around and were together for a couple of hours down by the river. It was just the one time, but apparently that's all it took. Nine months later..."

"You mean Belinda? You mean she's..."

"That's right, Daisy. Belinda is actually my daughter, not Ed's. It was never made public, and Belinda still doesn't know. But Beverly said that she just couldn't pass on to the next life without apologizing to Mary. I tried to tell her it would only cause damage, and rip apart lives, but she said that we should have been open about the affair from the beginning. I begged her for hours to just let things be, and she finally said she would think about it. About three weeks later, when Ira called nine-one-one about seeing Belinda and Charles taking your aunt out to the shed, I told the operator to consider the source, and ignore the call. Then I came out here, anyway, and found Beverly in here...tied up, unconcious, and barely breathing. I knew I couldn't take a chance on losing my beautiful wife, so I just took the opportunity to finish the job that Worman and Belinda thought they had completed.

"So you were plotting all along to frame them?"

"Now, hold on. They did poison her. They did think that they had killed her. So, they were going to jail anyway."

As the story rolled out, Daisy's mind became a mudhole. There was so much information to process...and surprises that she would have never dreamed possible. And as a result, she had, over the last several seconds, lowered her gun until it was only pointing at the floor. The sheriff took advantage of Daisy's confusion. He reached into his back pocket and grabbed a weapon that he had brought with him...a Taurus thirty-eight...and told her to drop her gun.

"Now, Daisy...this is the worst part of the whole thing. Up until now, I've been able to lay blame for your aunt's murder on two people who were already as guilty as me. But now that you know the story, I can't let you walk out of here alive. This is Charles Worman's gun...the same one he reported stolen...the same one that I took from his vehicle...the same one I used to shoot out the window of Jentz Randall's pick-up truck...and the same one that will be used to kill you. So our old buddy...Worm? Is that what you call him?...Our old buddy Worm is going to be found guilty of one more murder by the time I arrest him tomorrow afternoon."

"Sheriff...you wouldn't."

"Oh, but I would. I'm not going to prison, and I'm not going to lose Mary. Shooting you and framing that real estate guy is all I need to do." He raised the weapon and aimed at Daisy's head, a distance of only about four feet.

"I really am sorry, Daisy. There just isn't any other way."

At that time, a Marine busted open the door to the shed, and tackled the man with the gun. Jentz had no problem wrestling the revolver away from the surprised sheriff, and with a giant right fist, he delivered a blow to the jaw that rendered the villain completely unconscious. He immediately moved to embrace the beautiful blonde, who had been so shocked by the six-second encounter, she hadn't even had the presence of mind to let out a scream.

"Oh, Superman!...You came to my rescue again! Just in time, too. Ira's Starman was about to finish me off."

The sheriff was immediately secured with his own handcuffs, and then Deputy Parks was summoned to come and pick up his "trash." A middle-of-the-night meeting at Daisy's kitchen table broke the story to several who had been called, including Jentz' uncle Ray, Janey, the county attorney, and sadly, Mary Lundy.

According to plan, Charles and Belinda were arrested the following morning, although the charges were altered somewhat. They would eventually be sentenced for attempted murder, Sheriff Lundy would be found guilty of manslaughter, and the residents of Cade Valley would be talking about the whole affair for a very long time.

List of Key Characters

- Daisy Conrow – Lovely strong woman, returning home following a recent divorce
- John Hawkes – Daisy's womanizing ex-husband
- Janey – Owner of the local diner, family friend and confidante
- Mars Maxton – Former classmate of Daisy, and once-popular local football quarterback
- Charles Worman - Another former classmate, a well-known "nerd," now selling real estate
- Jentz Randall – A high school acquaintance of Daisy's, soon-to-be love interest
- Ray Franklin – Jentz' uncle, and owner of the hardware store
- Beverly Tipton – Daisy's beloved aunt who has gone missing
- Ed Tipton – Daisy's uncle (deceased for many years prior to this story)
- Belinda Tipton – Aunt Bev's wayward daughter (Daisy's cousin)
- Greta Barker – Rich girl in town with an eye on Jentz Randall
- Sheriff Lundy – Local law enforcement
- Mary Lundy – Sheriff's wife
- Parks – A deputy
- Briggs – A deputy
- Ira Berry – "Guest" at a nearby mental institution
- Brent Fuller – Owns the realty agency in the adjacent community

About the Author

Ron Reed Smith was born and reared in the Ozarks, where he still resides. Following a 38-year career in an aerospace industry, where most of his writing was dedicated to technical white papers, customer presentations, and product assembly instructions, Mr. Smith retired to create literature that was more entertaining and enjoyable. He is an author of non-fiction articles, short stories, and novella-length manuscripts. A review of his work will show that he enjoys tales with a clever twist and cozy mysteries. He has one multiple awards in both short-fiction and poetry categories.

He is a member of the Joplin Writers' Guild (Joplin, Missouri) and the Ozarks Writers League.

Printed in Great Britain
by Amazon

39775024R00066